The Tower R

Mary Grant Bruce

Alpha Editions

This edition published in 2024

ISBN : 9789357968850

Design and Setting By
Alpha Editions
www.alphaedis.com
Email - info@alphaedis.com

Contents

CHAPTER I I ANSWER AN ADVERTISEMENT ....- 1 -

CHAPTER II I BEGIN MY ADVENTURE ....- 8 -

CHAPTER III I MAKE A FRIEND...- 14 -

CHAPTER IV I DISCOVER MANY THINGS.......................- 21 -

CHAPTER V I WALK ABROAD AT NIGHT ....- 32 -

CHAPTER VI I MEET GOOD FORTUNE.............................- 38 -

CHAPTER VII I FIND SHEPHERD'S ISLAND ....- 50 -

CHAPTER VIII I HEAR STRANGE THINGS ....- 62 -

CHAPTER IX I BECOME A MEMBER OF THE BAND......- 71 -

CHAPTER X I HEAR OF ROBBERS ....- 78 -

CHAPTER XI I SEE DOUBLE ....- 84 -

CHAPTER XII I HEAR STRANGE CONFIDENCES............- 94 -

CHAPTER XIII I GO ADVENTURING ....- 100 -

CHAPTER XIV I FIND MYSELF A CONSPIRATOR ....- 106 -

CHAPTER XV I SAIL WITH MY BAND ....- 114 -

CHAPTER XVI I FIND A LUCKY SIXPENCE...................- 123 -

CHAPTER XVII I USE A POKER ....- 132 -

CHAPTER XVIII I LOSE MY SITUATION ....- 136 -

CHAPTER I
I ANSWER AN ADVERTISEMENT

NATURALLY it was not news to me when old Dr. Grayson told me I was tired. There are some things one knows without assistance: and for two months I had suspected that I was getting near the end of my tether. The twelve-year-olds I taught at school had become stupider and more stupid— or possibly I had; and Madame Carr—there was no real reason why she should be called "Madame," but that she thought it sounded better than plain "Mrs."—had grown stricter and more difficult to please. She had developed a habit of telling me, each afternoon, when school had been dismissed, what a low standard of deportment I exacted from my form. This also I knew; twelve-year-olds are not usually models of deportment, and I suppose I was not very awe-inspiring. But the daily information got on my nerves.

Then the examinations had been a nightmare. I used to wonder how the girls who grumbled at the questions would have liked the task of correcting the papers—taking bundles home at night and working at them after I had cooked the dinner and helped Colin to wash up. I made several mistakes, too; and of course Madame found them out. One is not at one's best, mentally, after a long day in school, and the little flat in Prahran was horribly hot and stuffy. Colin had wanted to help me, but of course I could not let him; the poor old boy used to work at his medical books every evening, in a wild hope that something might yet turn up to enable him to take his degree. I did my best at the wretched papers, but after an hour or so my head would ache until it really did not matter to me if I met the information that Dublin was situated on the Ganges. There had been a hideous interview with Madame after the breaking-up, in which she hinted, in an elephantine fashion, that unless my services were shown to be of more value she would hardly be justified in paying me as well as letting Madge have her education free.

It was scarcely a surprise, but, all the same, it staggered me. Housekeeping, since Father died, had not been an easy matter. Colin was just the best brother that ever lived, and when we found how little money there was for us, he had promptly left the University—he was in his fifth year, too, my poor boy. And how he loved the work! Father's practice brought something that we invested, and Colin got a position in an office. His salary was not much; he helped it out by working overtime whenever he could get the chance, and he had two pupils whom he coached for their second year. The big thing was that nothing must interfere with Madge's work.

Madge, you see, was the really brilliant one of the family: if we could keep her at school for another two years, she had a very good chance of a scholarship that would take her on to the University; and she had passed so many music exams that it would have been a tragedy not to have kept that up, too. I was not at all brilliant, and it seemed wonderful luck when Madame Carr offered me a minor post, at a small salary, with Madge's education thrown in. Of course, we knew that Madge was likely to be a very good advertisement for the school; still, it might not have happened, and that tiny salary of mine made all the difference in our finances. We managed, somehow—Colin and I; Madge could not be allowed to do any of the housework, for she was only fifteen, and she was working furiously. She fought us very hard about it, especially when we insisted that she should stay in bed to breakfast on Sunday mornings, but we were firm: so at last she gave in, more or less gracefully. And then I would find her sitting up in bed, darning my stockings. As I told her, it gave me quite a lot of extra work on Saturday night, hiding away everything she might possibly find to mend.

There never was anyone like Colin. He used to get up at some unearthly hour and do all the dirty work until it was time for him to rush to the office: and at night he helped just as cheerfully again. He was always cheerful; to see him washing-up you would have thought it was the thing he loved best on earth. I hated to see him scrubbing and polishing, with the long, slender hands that were just made for a doctor's. Nobody could imagine how good he was to me; and we managed as I said, somehow. But as I looked at Madame Carr's hard face I did not know how we could possibly manage without my little salary.

She relented a little towards the end of that unpleasant interview, and said she would think it over, and give me another chance; and she advised me to have a good rest, eat nourishing food, and take a few weeks in the hills. I suppose I must have looked pretty white, and she didn't want me to be ill there; at any rate, she said good-bye in a hurry, wished me a Merry Christmas, and hustled me off. I have no very clear memory of how I got down the hill to my train. But when I reached home I was idiotic enough to faint right off, which frightened poor Madge horribly, and sent her tearing to the nearest telephone for old Dr. Grayson, who had known us all our lives.

Dr. Grayson came, and was very kind, though his remarks were curiously like Madame's. He sounded me thoroughly, asked me innumerable questions, and finally told me there was nothing organically wrong—I was just tired, and needed rest and change. "Country air," he said cheerfully. "You won't get well in a back street in Prahran. Get away for a month—it's lucky that it is holiday time!" And he went off, airily oblivious of the fact that he might just as well have ordered me a trip to Mars.

It did not worry me much, although the bare idea of the country made me homesick. One expects doctors to say things, but it is not necessary to acquaint one's brother with all they say. Unfortunately, however, the old man met Colin on the doorstep, and must needs say it all over again to him; and Colin came in with the old worry-look in his eyes that I hated more than anything. I could hear him and Madge consulting in stage-whispers, in the kitchenette—they might have known that no variety of whisper can fail to be heard in a flat the size of ours, the four rooms of which would easily have fitted into our old dining-room at home. One could almost hear them adjusting the cheerful looks with which they presently came in.

They wouldn't let me do anything but lie on the sofa. Madge cooked the chops in a determined fashion that made the whole flat smell of burned fat; and Colin did everything else. After dinner was over—it was a gruesome meal, at which Colin was laboriously funny all the time—I was graciously allowed to sit in the kitchenette while they washed up, and we held a council of war.

All the talking in the world could not alter the main fact. There were no funds to pay for country holidays. Our friends—they were not so many as in the old days—were all in Melbourne: our only relations were distant ones, distant in every sense of the word, for they lived in Queensland, and might as well have been in Timbuctoo, Madge sourly remarked, for all the practical use they were. Discuss it as we might, there was no earthly chance of following my prescription.

Poor old Colin looked more like thirty-three than twenty-three as he scrubbed the gridiron with sand-soap.

"You needn't worry yourselves a bit," I told them. "All I need is to be away from that horrid old school and Madame Carr, and I've got two whole beautiful months. Doctors don't know everything. I'll go and sit in Fawkner Park every day and look at the cows, and imagine I'm in Gippsland!"

Colin groaned.

"I don't see why we haven't a country uncle or something," said Madge vaguely: "a red-faced old darling with a loving heart, and a red-roofed farm, and a beautiful herd of cows—Wyandottes, don't you call them? If we were girls in books we'd have one, and we'd go and stay with him and get hideously fat, and Doris would marry the nearest squatter!" She heaved a sigh.

"Hang the squatter!" Colin remarked; "but I'd give something to see either of you fat. I'm afraid you're a vain dreamer, Madge. Put down that dish-cloth and let me finish: I'm not going to have you showing up at a music-lesson with hands like a charlady's."

Madge gave up the dish-cloth with reluctance. She was silent for quite three minutes—an unusual thing for Madge.

"Look here," she said at length, with a funny little air of determination. "There's one thing a whole lot more important than music, and that's Doris's health. I wonder we didn't think of it before!"

"Well, I'd hate to contradict you," Colin answered, slightly puzzled. "But I don't see that this highly-original discovery of yours makes it any the more necessary for you to scour saucepans while I'm about."

"Oh, bother the saucepans!" said Madge impatiently. "I didn't mean that—though it's more my work than yours to wash them, anyhow. Washing-up isn't a man's job."

"There isn't any man-and-woman business about this establishment," said Colin firmly, "except that I'm boss. Just get that clearly in your young mind. And what did you mean, if you meant anything?"

"Why, it's as clear as daylight," Madge announced. "Doris's health is more important than music: you admitted that yourself. Well, then, let's sell the piano!"

We looked at each other in blank amazement. Sell the piano! Madge's adored piano, Father's last gift to her. Beneath her fingers it was a very wonder-chest of magic and delight: all the fairies of laughter, all the melody of rippling water, all the dearest dreams come true were there when Madge played. Already old Ferrari, her Italian music-master, talked to us of triumphs ahead—triumphs in a wider field than Australia. And she sat on the kitchen table, swinging her legs, and talked of selling her Bechstein! No wonder we gasped.

"Talk sense!" growled Colin, when his breath came back.

"It *is* sense," Madge retorted. "It's worth ever so much money: a cheaper piano would do me just as well to practise on. Even if I gave up music altogether it would be worth it to give Doris a rest. She can't go on as she is—you can see that for yourself, Colin Earle!"

"I certainly can't go on hearing you rave!" I said. "Why, when you're a second Paderewski you have got to be the prop of our declining years. It would be just about the finish for Colin and me if your music were interfered with, and——" at which point I suddenly found something hard in my throat. I suppose it was because I was a bit tired, for we aren't a weepy family, but I just howled.

It alarmed Colin and Madge very badly. They patted me on the back and assured me I shouldn't be bothered in any way, and begged me to drink some water: and when I managed to get hold of my voice again I seized the opportunity to make Madge promise that she wouldn't mention the word "selling" in connection with the Bechstein again, unless we were really at our last gasp. This accomplished, we dispatched her to practice, and Colin returned to the washing-up.

Madge went, rather reluctantly, and Colin rubbed away at the saucepans, with the furrow deepening between his brows. I was in the midst of explaining clearly to him that I did not need a change, quite conscious the while of my utter failure to convince him, when there was a clatter in the passage, and Madge burst in, waving a newspaper, and incoherent with excitement.

"What on earth is the matter with the kid?" Colin asked, a little wearily. "Do go easy, Madge, and say what you want to, when you have finished brandishing that paper in your lily hand. Meanwhile, get off my sand-soap." He rescued it, and turned a critical eye on the bottom of a saucepan. We were more or less used to Madge's outbreaks, but to-night they seemed to be taking an acute form.

"It's the very thing!" she cried, the words tumbling over each other. "Just what we want, and it's in this morning's paper, so I don't suppose anyone has got it yet, and now she'll really get fat, and you needn't be scornful, Colin, so there!"

"I'm not," said Colin. "But I'd love to know what it's all about."

"Why, this advertisement," said Madge excitedly. "Listen, you two:

> Lady requiring rest and change offered pleasant country home, few weeks, return light services. Teacher preferred. References exchanged."

There followed an address in the south-west of Victoria.

"Oh, get out!" Colin said. "Doris doesn't want to leave off work to carry bricks!"

"But it says 'light services,' don't you see?" protested Madge. "There might not be much to do at all—not more than enough to keep her from 'broodin' on bein' a dorg'! And she'd get rest and change. It says so. And 'references exchanged'—it's so beautifully circumspect." Our youngest put on a quaint little air of being at least seventy-five. "Personally, I think it was made for Doris!"

"You always had a sanguine mind," was Colin's comment on this attitude. "What does the patient think about it?"

"I'm not a patient," I contradicted. "But—I don't know—it sounds as if it might be all right, Colin. The 'pleasant country home' sounds attractive. I wouldn't mind any ordinary housework, if they were nice people."

"But they might be beasts," said my brother pithily. "I don't feel like letting you risk it." He paused, frowning. "Wish I knew which might be the greater risk. There's no doubt that you ought to get away from here."

"Well, write for particulars—and references," suggested Madge. "No harm in that, at all events."

Colin pondered heavily.

"I believe the kid has made an illuminating remark," he said at length. "You don't commit yourself by writing: perhaps it would be as well to give it a trial. Though I wouldn't dream of it for a moment if I saw the remotest chance of sending you out of Melbourne in any other way, old white-face!" He put his arm round my shoulders as we went into the dining-room—which was very unusual for Colin, and affected me greatly. I began to wonder was I consumptive or something, but cheered up on remembering that the doctor had said I was "organically sound."

I wrote my letter, enclosing a testimonial from Dr. Grayson, as to my general worth; he was very kind, and drew so touching a picture of my character and capabilities that I was quite certain in my own mind I could never live up to it. I told him so, after he made me read it, but he would not alter it, and threatened me with all kinds of pains and penalties if I failed to prove every word he had said about me. After that, it seemed scarcely prudent to ask Madame Carr for a letter—the difference between my two "references" might have been too marked. Much to Madge's disgust, I insisted on telling my prospective employer that I was only eighteen. This excited the gloomiest forebodings in my sister.

"You'll queer your pitch altogether," she said. "Eighteen's awfully young; ten to one she wants an old frump of thirty!"

"Well, if she does, she had better not have me," said I. "I don't want her to expect some one old and staid, and then have heart-failure when she sees my extreme youth."

"Perhaps not," Madge agreed reluctantly. "Everything depends on first impressions, and I suppose heart-failure wouldn't be the best possible beginning. Anyhow, you might say that you're five feet eight and not shingled. That would give her a vision of some one impressive and dignified."

"Then she might get a different kind of shock," I said. "But I don't think we need worry; you may be certain that she'll have dozens and dozens of applications, and it isn't a bit likely that she will want me. I'm going to forget all about it, as soon as the letter has gone—and you can look out for other advertisements. It's foolish to expect to catch your fish the moment you throw in the first bait."

"I'm not at all certain that I want to catch her," said Colin gloomily. "It's not much fun to catch your fish and find you've hooked a shark!"

CHAPTER II
I BEGIN MY ADVENTURE

THE letter went, and we waited for a reply: Madge feverishly, I apathetically, and Colin with a good deal of unhappy anticipation: he hated the whole business. I know the poor boy made frantic efforts during those days to earn some extra money, and he did manage to secure some overtime from a fellow-clerk who did not want it. But of course it was very little.

"If I could only rake up enough to send you for a fortnight to Frankston!" he said one evening. "That would be absolute rest for you; far better than slogging at alleged 'light duties' in some strange house. I can't stick the idea of your going away to work, Dor."

"But I'm quite able to work—truly, old boy," I told him. "It was only the long hours in school that knocked me up, and the rush every morning."

"And that will be just the same after the holidays," he growled. It was quite amazing to hear Colin growl: he had always been so cheery over our misfortunes, and had never once shown that he minded his own bitter disappointment. "If only I could earn enough to keep you at home! I believe it would be more sensible if I worked as a dock labourer: I'd make more money then, and my own expenses would be hardly anything."

"Yes, and then a strike would come along, and you would go out with your Union, and we should be worse off than ever," I said practically. "I wish you wouldn't talk such absolute nonsense. I only needed a rest, which I'm getting now. Don't I look ever so much fitter already?"

"You do look a bit less like a scarecrow," he admitted. "But I know that you're not getting the nourishing things the doctor ordered, and you ought to be right away from Melbourne. January in Prahran isn't going to be any sort of a picnic for you."

"When I have finished that bottle of Burgundy you brought home yesterday you won't know me," I said. "Just you wait, and don't worry. Something may turn up at any time; and meanwhile, I'm going to spend every day in the Gardens or on the beach. Isn't it lucky that it costs so little to get to them?" But all my well-meant efforts failed to cheer him much. He got into a way of looking at me, with his forehead all wrinkled with worry, that made me positively ache for a favourable answer from the advertisement lady. Without telling him or Madge, I went into Melbourne and spent a weary afternoon going round the registry-offices in search of a holiday job in the country. But no one seemed to have the least desire for my services except as a "general." There, indeed, I could have had my pick of hungry employers, only I didn't dare to meet them—with the prospect of facing Colin afterwards.

Christmas came and went, and we gave up all idea of getting any answer to my letter. It was a very small Christmas we had—just sandwiches and a thermos of coffee in a quiet corner of the Botanical Gardens, watching the dabchicks in the lake, and building all sorts of castles for the future. We made a solemn compact that no one should worry during the day, and Colin kept to it nobly and played the fool all the time. So it was really a very jolly Christmas, and we all felt better for it.

On Boxing Day Colin wanted to spring-clean the flat; but at that point Madge and I felt we must put our collective feet down, and we did. So we packed the basket again, and went to one of the nearer beaches—one where it is still possible to find quiet corners in the scrub: and we bathed and picnicked, and enjoyed watching Colin smoke the cigarettes we had given him for Christmas—after Father died he had given up smoking, declaring that it made his head ache. It was beautiful to see how peaceful he looked. Altogether, the Earle family agreed that it was probable that a good many people had not enjoyed the holidays as much as we did.

And the next day came the answer to my letter—just as we had given up all hope.

It arrived by the evening post, which was late. Colin had come home, and we knew what it was by the way Madge came clattering along the corridor and burst into the flat. She waved a thick white envelope round her head.

"It's her!" she shouted. "I know it is!"

"I wish Madame could hear you," I said. "Is it for me?"

"Of course it is. Doesn't it look opulent and splendid! Hurry up and open it, Doris, or I'll explode!"

My fingers were a little shaky as I tore open the envelope and read the letter aloud:

"DEAR MISS EARLE,—

"I have received several letters in answer to my advertisement, but, after consideration, yours seems the most suitable. I require a lady in my home for a few weeks, to take off my hands some of the duties of caring for a house-party, and to assist in looking after my younger children during the absence of their governess, who is away on holiday. As the employment is light, I offer a salary of £1 per week, and would pay your travelling expenses to and from Melbourne.

"I have hesitated in accepting your application because you are very young."

"I *told* you so!" breathed Madge disgustedly.

"However, your testimonial is excellent; and the teaching experience to which it alludes should enable you to control the children. I trust that you are firm and tactful."

"Firm and tactful!—I like that!" uttered Colin. "Will she let you control the little beasts with a stick?"

"Be quiet—there's more yet. 'My house is large, and I keep three maids. A dinner-dress is advisable, should you have one. If you decide to come to me, I should like you to leave Melbourne on the second of January.'" And she was mine faithfully, Marie McNab.

"Born—or christened, rather—plain Mary, I'll bet," was Colin's comment. "What's the enclosure?"

The enclosure was the "references exchanged": a vague sort of assurance from the clergyman in Wootong that Mrs. McNab of "The Towers" was all that she ought to be. Colin remarked that it seemed to deal more with her religious beliefs than her ideas on feeding-up tired assistants, which latter was the point on which he was more curious; but he supposed it was all right. And then he and Madge sat and looked at me, waiting for me to speak.

"I think I'll go," I said, when the silence was becoming oppressive. "There can be no harm in trying—and, thank goodness, it doesn't cost anything."

"The old cat might have offered you a bit more screw," said Madge, with that extreme elegance of diction which marks the college girl. "Apparently she's wading in wealth—three maids, and lives in Towers, and has a crest as big as your head on her notepaper. Flamboyant display, I call it. How about striking for more pay after you get there?"

"Not done," said Colin. "Doris doesn't belong to a Union. I say, Dor, have you got enough clothes for living in Towers?"

"Oh, they'll do, I think," I answered; "there's some advantage of being in half-mourning. I shall have to fix up a few little things, but not much. Shoes are the worst; I do need a new pair. My brown ones are put away; old Hoxon can stain them black for me."

Madge sighed.

"I hate blacked-up brown," she said. "And they were such pretty shoes, Dor."

"I can get new ones when you are a learned professor," I told her, laughing. "And you'll be that in a year or two, if you leave off slang. Gloves are an item—thank goodness we take the same size, and I can borrow from you!"

Madge echoed my gratitude. She hated gloves.

"And you may have my big hat," she said—"it's just the sort of hat you may need in the country. And my dressing-jacket; I'll bet that will impress the three maids!"

"My dear, I'm not going to rob you in that wholesale fashion," I said. "Also, I don't contemplate parading before the staff in my dressing-jacket—in the servants' hall, I suppose. Possibly there is a chauffeur, too!"

"Well, he'd love it," Madge grinned. "All chauffeurs have an eye for clothes; and it's such a pretty blue. I wish you could wear it in to dinner. What *will* you wear for dinner, by the way, my child?"

"I'll have to get out my old lace frock. It's quite good, and I can make it look all right with a little touching-up. Then there's my black *crêpe de Chine*: so suitable and dowagerish. Mrs. McNab will approve of it, I'm sure. I know I could control the children well in black *crêpe de Chine*!"

In which I spoke without knowing the Towers children. The words were to come back to me later.

"What a mercy we've got decent luggage!" said Madge. "I'd hate you to face battlemented Towers and proud chauffeurs with shabby suitcases."

I echoed her thankfulness. Father had brought us up to think that there was nothing like leather; our trunks, even as the Bechstein piano, were among the few relics of a past in which money had never seemed to be a consideration. It was comforting to think that one need not face the unknown McNabs with a dress-basket.

Then Colin spoke.

"You've made up your mind to go, then, Doris?"

I looked at him. I knew how he hated it all.

"Don't you think it is best, old boy?"

"Oh, I suppose so," he said half savagely. He got up, looking for his hat. Presently the door of the flat banged behind him.

I was glad when the next few days were over. They went with a rush, for I was terribly busy: even if you are in half-mourning, and you think your clothes are pretty well in order, you are sure to find heaps to do when it comes to going away. Madge helped me like an angel; worked early and late, took all the housekeeping off my shoulders, and found time to do ever so many bits of mending. Between us, we just managed enough clothes; as Madge said, it was very fortunate that her only wish was to live the simple life during the holidays; but I felt horribly mean to take her things. Still, I did not see what else to do. One must be clad.

We puzzled a good deal over what I should and should not take. Music had not been mentioned by Mrs. McNab, but it seemed as well to put in a little; and I found corners for a few of my best-beloved books, in case the Towers should be barren in that respect. I looked longingly at my golf-clubs, not used for eighteen months, with all their lovely heads tied up in oily flannel. But I decided they were not in keeping with my situation. I had an instinctive belief that my light duties would not include golf. My tennis racket went in—but well at the bottom of my trunk, where I thought it highly probable it would remain throughout my stay at The Towers.

I packed on New Year's night, with Colin and Madge both sitting on my bed, offering flippant advice. Colin had spoken very little since Mrs. McNab's letter had come, and I knew he was making a violent effort to "buck up." Not that he had not always been a dear; but he could not bear the idea of my going to strangers in such a way. He had come home on New Year's Eve with the loveliest pair of shoes for me. I don't know how he had managed to buy them—and they were such good ones, too, the very sort my soul loved. I nearly cried when he gave them to me; and he patted me on the back, very hard. He made me go to bed as soon as the packing was over, and Madge brewed cocoa and made toast, with a spendthrift lavishness of butter. We all had a midnight supper on my bed. I often thought of that light-hearted supper in the days that followed. It was very cheerful, and we drank the health of everybody, including Mrs. McNab and the cat.

It was all a rush next morning. The carrier came very early for my trunk, and I rushed round making final preparations and packing my little suit-case. There seemed ever so much to say at the last moment. Madge was quite cross with me because I stopped when I was putting on my hat to tell her how to thicken soup. Just as I was ready to make a dash for the train, to my joy Colin appeared—he had got an hour off from the office, and had raced home to carry my things for me and save me any trouble. They put me into the train at Spencer Street, and Colin recklessly flung magazines and sweets into my lap. I have always said that few could adorn riches better than Colin—his ideas are so comfortable.

Then they hugged me vigorously, and the guard shouted "Stand clear!" and the train started.

Colin ran alongside the window as long as he could.

"Mind—you're to come back at once if it isn't all right," he said authoritatively. "You understand, Doris?" I nodded—I couldn't speak. Then the porter yelled angrily at Colin, and he dropped back. I leaned out until the train went round the curve, while he and Madge stood waving on the platform.

I cried a little at first—I couldn't help it. I had never been away by myself before; it was so suddenly lonely, and they had been such dears to me. It was not pleasant, either, to picture little Madge going back to the flat by herself, to tidy up; then to spend all the afternoon, until Colin came home, over dull old lesson-books. And I knew Colin would miss me: we were such chums. I was missing him horribly already.

After awhile I cheered up. The thing had to be, and I might as well make the best of it, and remember that my whole duty in life, according to Madge, was to get fat. The country was pretty, too: it had been a wet season, and all the paddocks were green and fresh, and the cattle and sheep looked beautiful. Fate had made Father a doctor, but he had always said that his heart lay in farming, and I had inherited his tastes. To Colin and Madge a bullock was merely something that produced steak, but to me it was a thing of beauty. It was so long since I had been for any kind of a journey that the mere travelling was a pleasure. Mrs. McNab had sent money for a first-class fare, which we all thought very decent of her: she had explained in a stiff little note that she did not approve of young girls travelling alone second-class. Colin had snorted, remarking that he had never had the slightest intention of letting me do so: but it was decent, all the same. I sent her a brainwave of thanks as I leaned back in comfort, glad to rest after the racket of the last few days. I did not even want to read my magazines, though a new magazine was unfamiliar enough to us, nowadays, to be a treat. It was delightful to watch the country, to do nothing, to enjoy the luxury of having the compartment to myself.

That lasted for nearly half the journey. Then, just as the engine whistled and the train began to move slowly out of a little station, a porter flung open the door hurriedly, and some one dashed in, stumbling over my feet, and distributing golf-clubs, fishing-rods, and other loose impedimenta about the carriage. The porter hurled through the window other articles—a stick, a kit-bag, an overcoat; and the new-comer, leaning out, tossed him something that rattled loudly on the platform. Then he sat down and panted.

CHAPTER III
I MAKE A FRIEND

"I BEG your pardon for tumbling over you in such a way," he said. "Awfully rude of me—but I hadn't time to think. The car went wrong, and I never thought we'd catch the train—had to sprint the last two hundred yards. I do hope I didn't hurt you?"

He was a tall young man with the nicest ugly face I had ever seen. His hair was red, and he was liberally freckled: he had a nondescript nose, a mouth of large proportions, and quite good blue eyes. He seemed to hang together loosely. There was something so friendly about his face that I found myself answering his smile almost as if he were Colin.

"No, you didn't hurt me," I told him. "I would have moved out of the way if I hadn't been dreaming—but I had no time."

"I should think you hadn't!" he said, laughing. "It was the most spectacular entry I ever made. But I'd have hated to miss the train."

I murmured something vaguely polite, and relapsed into silence, bearing in mind the fact that well-brought-up young persons do not talk in railway carriages to strange men, even if the said men have fallen violently over their feet. My fellow-traveller became silent, too, though I felt him glance at me occasionally. The placid content which had seemed to fill the carriage was gone, and I began to feel tired. I read a magazine, wishing the journey would end.

Presently we stopped in a large station, and the red-haired man disappeared. He was back in a few moments, looking a little sheepish, as one who is afraid of his reception.

"I've brought you a cup of tea," he said—"please don't mind. You look awfully tired, and you've a long way to go yet. I read the address on your suit-case." He cast a glance towards the rack, and held out the cup meekly.

My training in etiquette had not covered this emergency, and I hesitated. But he was so boyish and friendly—just as Colin would have been—and so evidently afraid of being snubbed, that I couldn't hurt him; and also I wanted the tea very badly. It was quite good tea, too, and the scone that accompanied it was a really superior one.

I felt much better when I had finished, and my fellow-traveller came back for my cup, which he presented to a porter, for the train was about to start.

"Girls are so various," said he, sitting down opposite me, with his friendly smile. "Some would hate you to offer them tea, and some would hate you not to, and some would be just nice about it. I felt certain you belonged to the third lot! It's such a beastly long way to Wootong, too: I'm going there myself, so I suppose that might be considered a sort of introduction. And you looked just about knocked-up. Know Wootong well?"

"I've never been there," I said. "I'm going to a place called The Towers."

"What!—the McNabs?" exclaimed my companion. "But how ripping!—I'm going there myself. I'm Dick Atherton; Harry McNab and I share rooms at Trinity. I don't think I've met you there before, have I? No, of course, what an ass I am: you said it was your first visit."

"I'm hardly a visitor," I said. It wasn't easy, but I thought it best to have things on a straight footing. "I'm . . ." It came to me suddenly that I hardly knew *what* I was. "I'm—a sort of governess, I suppose. I'm going up, just for the holidays, to help Mrs. McNab."

"What a shame!" said Mr. Atherton promptly—apparently, before taking thought. He pulled himself up, reddening. "At least—you know what I mean. Those kids ought to have some one about six feet, and weighing quite twelve stone, to keep them in order. They're outlaws. Anyway, I'm sure to see an awful lot of you, if you'll let me. Won't you tell me what to call you?"

I told him, and we chatted on cheerfully. He was the most transparent person possible, and though I am not considered astute—by Colin and Madge, who should know—it was quite easy to find out from him a good deal about my new post. I inferred that my appearance might be a shock to Mrs. McNab, whose previous assistants had been more of the type graphically depicted by Mr. Atherton—he referred to them simply as "the cats." Also, the children seemed to be something of a handful. There were two, a boy and a girl, besides the brother at Trinity—and a grown-up sister. It was only when I angled for information on the subject of Mrs. McNab that my companion evaded the hook.

"She writes, you know," he said, vaguely. I said I hadn't known, and looked for further particulars.

" 'Fraid I haven't read any of her books," said the boy. "I suppose I should, as I go to stay there: but I'm not much of a chap for reading, unless it's American yarns—you know, cowboy stuff. I can tackle those: but Mrs. McNab's would be a bit beyond me. I tried an article of hers once, in a magazine my sister had, but even a wet towel round my head couldn't make it anything but Greek to me. And the Prof. could tell you how much good I am at Greek!"

"She writes real books, then?" I asked, greatly thrilled. I had never met anyone who actually wrote books, and in my innocence it seemed to me that authors must be wholly wonderful.

"Oh, rather! She's 'Julia Smale,' you see. Ever heard of her?"

I had—in a vague way: had even encountered a book by "Julia Smale," lent me by a fellow-teacher at Madame Carr's, who had passed it on to me with the remark that if I could make head or tail of it, it was more than she had been able to do. I had found it a novel of the severe type, full of reflections that were far too deep for me. With a sigh for having wasted an opportunity that might be useful, I remembered that I had not finished it. How I wished that I had done so! It would have been such an excellent introduction to my employer, I thought, if I could have lightly led the conversation to this masterpiece in the first half-hour at The Towers. Now, I could only hope that she would never mention it.

Mr. Atherton nodded sympathetically as I confided this to him.

"I'm blessed if I know anyone who does read them," he said. "They may be the sort of thing the Americans like: she publishes in America, you know. Curious people, the Yanks: you wouldn't think that the nation that can produce a real good yarn like 'The Six-Gun Tenderfoot' would open its heart to 'Julia Smale.' I'm quite sure Harry and Beryl—that's her daughter—don't read her works. Certainly, I'll say for her she doesn't seem to expect anyone to. She locks herself up alone to write, and nobody dares to disturb her, but she doesn't talk much about the work. Not like a Johnny I knew who wrote a book; he used to wander down Collins Street with it in his hand, and asked every soul he knew if they'd read it. Very trying, because it was awful bosh, and nobody had. Mrs. McNab isn't like that, thank goodness!"

"And Mr. McNab?" I asked.

"Oh, he's a nice old chap. Not so old, either, when I come to think of it: I believe they were married very young. A bit hard, they say, but a good sort. He's away: sailed for England last month, on a year's trip."

I did not like to ask any more questions, so the conversation switched on to something else, and the time went by quite quickly. The train was a slow one, crawling along in a leisurely fashion and stopping for lengthy periods at all the little stations; it would have been a dull journey alone, and I was glad of my cheery red-haired companion. By the time we reached Wootong we were quite old friends; and any feeling that I might have had about the informality of our introduction to each other was completely dissolved by the discovery that he had a wholesome reverence for Colin's reputation in athletics, which was apparently a sort of College tradition. When Mr. Atherton found that I was "the" Earle's sister he gazed at me with a reverence which I fear had never been excited by Mrs. McNab, even in her most literary moments. It was almost embarrassing, but not unpleasing: and we talked of Colin and his school and college record until we felt that we had known each other for years. I didn't know whether to be glad or sorry when, after a long run, the train slackened speed, and Mr. Atherton began hurriedly to collect our luggage, remarking, "By George, we're nearly in!" And a moment later I was standing, a little forlornly, on the Wootong platform.

Two girls were waiting, both plump and pretty, and very smart—perhaps a shade too smart for the occasion, but very well turned-out. They greeted my companion joyfully, and there was a little babel of chatter, while I stood apart, hardly knowing what to do. Then I heard one of the girls break off suddenly.

"We've got to collect one of Mother's cats," she said, not lowering her voice at all. "Seen anything of her, Dicky? She was to come on this train."

Mr. Atherton turned as red as his hair. I had already done so.

"S-sh!" he said. "Steady, Beryl—she'll hear you." Apparently he thought I should not hear him, but there wasn't any escaping his voice. He came over to me, and conducted me across the platform. "This is Miss Earle, whom you are to collect," he told her. "Miss Beryl McNab, Miss Earle—and Miss Guest."

Neither girl proffered a hand, and I was wildly thankful for the impulse that had kept mine by my side. Instead, there was blank amazement on their faces.

"Then you've known each other before?" Beryl McNab said.

"No—I introduced myself on the way down," explained Mr. Atherton hurriedly. "Tumbled into Miss Earle's compartment, and fell violently over her; and then I found she was coming here. It was great luck for me."

"Quite so," said the elder girl; and there was something in her tone that made me shrivel. "I needn't ask if you had a pleasant journey, Miss Earle. If you're ready, we can start: the cart will bring your luggage." We all went out to a big blue motor, manned by a chauffeur who came up to all Madge's forecasts; and whisked away along a winding road fringed with poplar-trees and hawthorn hedges.

Mr. Atherton made gallant attempts to include me in the conversation, but there was a weight on my spirits, and I gave him back monosyllables: I hope they were polite ones. The girls did not worry about me at all. They chatted in a disjointed fashion, but I was quite ignored. This, I realized, was the proper status of "a cat" at The Towers; probably a shade more marked in my case, because I was a young cat, and had sinned. Deeply did I regret that a friend of the family should have hurtled into my carriage: bitterly I repented that welcome cup of tea. It seemed ages, though it was really less than ten minutes, before we turned into a big paddock, where, half a mile ahead, a grey house showed among the box-trees fringing a hill.

We skimmed up a long drive, skirted a wide lawn where several people were having tea under a big oak, and stopped before the hall-door. A short, thick-set youth in a Trinity blazer, who was tormenting a fox-terrier on the veranda, uttered a shout of welcome and precipitated himself upon Mr. Atherton, who thumped him affectionately on the back. Then there came racing through the hall a boy and girl of twelve and fourteen, ridiculously alike; and beneath their joyful onslaught the guest was temporarily submerged. Nobody took the slightest notice of me until a tall angular woman in a tailor-made frock came striding along the veranda, and, after greeting her son's friend, glanced inquiringly in my direction.

"Oh—this is Miss Earle, Mother," Beryl McNab said. "She and Dicky came down together."

There was evident surprise in my employer's face as she looked me over. She gave me a limp hand.

"Then you and Mr. Atherton have met before?" she asked.

Dicky Atherton rushed into his explanation, which sounded, I must admit, fairly unconvincing. I was conscious of a distinct drop in the temperature: certainly Mrs. McNab's voice had frozen perceptibly when she spoke again.

"How curious!" she said: I had not imagined that two words could make one feel so small and young. "You have met my daughter, of course: this is my eldest son, and Judith and Jack are your especial charges."

The college youth favoured me with a long stare, and the boy and girl with a short one. Then Judith smiled with exceeding sweetness and put out her hand.

"I wish you luck!" she said solemnly.

There was a general ripple of laughter.

"Miss Earle will need all the luck she can get if she's to manage you two imps," said Harry McNab, shaking hands. "You might as well realize, Miss Earle, that it can't be done: at least no one has succeeded yet in making them decent members of society."

Mrs. McNab interposed.

"Don't talk nonsense, Harry," she said, severely. "If you will come with me, Miss Earle, I will show you your room." She led the way into the house, and I followed meekly, my heart in my shoes.

A huge square hall, furnished as a sitting-room, opened at one end into a conservatory. From one corner ascended a splendidly-carved staircase, with wide, shallow steps, which formed, above, a gallery that ran round two sides of the hall. Up this I trailed at my employer's heels, and, passing down a softly-carpeted passage, found myself in a room at the end; small, but pleasant enough, with a large window overlooking the back premises and part of the garden. Beyond the back yard came a stretch of lightly-timbered paddock, which ended abruptly in what, I found later on, was a steep descent to the beach. The shore itself was hidden from the house by the edge of the cliff: but further out showed the deep-blue line of the sea, broken by curving headlands that formed the bay near which The Towers stood. It was all beautiful; in any other circumstances I should have been wildly happy to be in such a place. But as it was, I longed for the little back street in Prahran!

Mrs. McNab was speaking in her cool, hard voice.

"This is your room, Miss Earle. Judith's is next door, and Jack's just across the passage. Judith will show you the schoolroom, which will be your sitting-room, later on. You will generally have your evening meal there with the children. To-morrow I will take you over the house and explain your duties to you. You are probably tired after your journey; I will send you up some tea, and then you had better rest until the evening."

The words were kind enough, but the voice would have chilled anyone. I stammered out something in the way of thanks, and Mrs. McNab went out, her firm tread sounding briskly along the passage. Presently a neat maid brought in a tray and put it down with a long stare at me—a stare compounded equally of superciliousness and curiosity; and I was left alone in my new home.

" 'I've brought you a cup of tea,' he said—
'please don't mind. You look awfully tired.' "
The Tower Rooms]

CHAPTER IV
I DISCOVER MANY THINGS

TWO days later I had settled down fairly well to life at The Towers.

My responsibilities were varied. It was mine to superintend the early toilet of Judith and Jack: mine to keep a watchful eye on the vagaries of the parlourmaid, who was given to dreaming when laying the table, and possessed a disregard, curious in one of her calling, for the placing of correct spoons and forks. She admitted her limitations, but nevertheless deeply resented my existence. I arranged flowers in all the sitting-rooms, gave out linen, prepared picnic luncheons and teas, cut sandwiches, helped to pick fruit, saw that trains were met whenever necessary, wrote letters for Mrs. McNab, played accompaniments or dance-music when desired, did odd jobs of mending, and, in short, was required to be always on hand and never in evidence. Incidentally and invariably, there were Judith and Jack.

They were a curious pair, alike in appearance and character; untamed young savages in many ways, but with a kind of rough honesty that did much to redeem their pranks. I used to wonder what was their attitude towards their father; it would have been a comfort to think that they paid him any reverence, for it was a quality conspicuously lacking in their dealings with anyone else. Their mother made spasmodic efforts to control them, generally ending with a resigned shrug and a sigh. For the greater part of each day they pursued their own sweet will, unchecked. Never had I met two youngsters so urgently needing the common sense discipline of a good boarding-school, and it rejoiced me to learn that after the holidays this was to be their portion; since their governess, after leaving for her holidays, had decided that she was not equal to the task of facing them again, and had written to resign her position. Judy and Jack rejoiced openly. I inferred, indeed, that they had deliberately laboured towards this end.

That the pair had a reputation for evil ways, and were determined to uphold it, was plain to me from my first evening in the house. They regarded every one as fair game: but the "holiday governess" was their especial prey, and, so far as I could gather, their treatment of the species partook of the nature of vivisection. Ostensibly, we were supposed to be a good deal together, for I found that I was invariably expected to know where they were; but as my duties kept me busy for the greater part of the day, and the children were wont to follow their own devices, we seldom foregathered much before afternoon tea, for which function I wildly endeavoured to produce them seemly clad. We dined together in the schoolroom at night, and afterwards descended decorously to the drawing-room for an hour—if they did not give me the slip; and Mrs. McNab had conveyed to me that there was no need for me to sit up after their bed-time. It was this considerate hint that made me realize what my employer meant by "rest and change."

On that first evening I had my introduction to the merry characteristics of Judy and Jack. Mrs. McNab had excused us from attendance in the drawing-room, at which they had uttered yells of joy, forthwith racing down the kitchen stairs to parts unknown. It did not seem worth while to follow them, so I sat in the schoolroom, writing a letter to Colin and Madge. I spread myself on description in that letter: Madge told me later on that my eye for scenery had amazed them both. I hoped the letter sounded more cheerful than I felt. But the writing of it made me more homesick than ever, and when I had finished there seemed nothing worth doing except to go to bed.

The sight of my room brought me up all standing. My luggage had come up too late for me to do more than begin unpacking: and Judy and Jack had been before me to complete the task. The engaging pair had literally "made hay" of my possessions. My trunk stood empty, its contents littering the floor; the bedposts were dressed in my raiment and crowned with my hats, my shoes were knotted and buckled together in a wild heap on the bed. On the table stood my three photographs—Father, Colin, and Madge; each turned upside down in its frame. There was no actual damage: merely everything that an impish ingenuity could suggest. It was apparent that they had enjoyed themselves very much.

I was very tired, and my first impulse was of wild wrath, followed swiftly by an almost uncontrollable desire to cry. Happily, I had sufficient backbone left to check myself. I walked across the room, rescued a petticoat which fluttered, flag-wise, from the window, attached to my umbrella, and began to reverse the photographs. As I did so, I heard a low giggle at the door.

"Come in," I said politely. "Don't be frightened."

There was a moment's pause, a whispered colloquy, and two flushed faces appeared.

"We're not frightened," said Judy defiantly.

"So glad—why should you be?" I asked cheerfully. "Sit down, won't you?—if you can find a space." I took up Colin's outraged photograph and adjusted it with fingers that itched for a cane, and for power to use it.

"That your young man, Miss Earle?" Jack asked, nudging Judy.

"That is my brother," I said.

"Oh! What does he do?"

"He does a good many things," I answered. "He used to be pretty good at athletics at school and Trinity."

"I say!—was your brother at Trinity? Why, Harry's there!"

"He was," I said. "He was a medical student when this was taken."

Sudden comprehension lit Judy's face.

"Not Earle who was captain of the university football team?"

"Yes."

"By Jupiter!" Jack uttered. "Why, I've read about him—he's the chap they call 'the record-breaker.' My word, I'd like to know him!"

"Would you?" I remarked pleasantly, polishing Colin's photograph diligently with my handkerchief. "Perhaps you and he wouldn't agree very well if you did meet; there are some things my brother would call 'beastly bad form.' He is rather particular."

There was dead silence, and my visitors turned very red. Then Jack mumbled something about helping me to tidy up, and the pair fell upon my property. Jack disentangled my shoes while Judy unclothed the bedposts: together they crawled upon the floor picking up stockings and handkerchiefs, and laying them in seemly piles; and I sat in the one chair the room boasted and polished Colin's photograph. It was excessively bright when my pupils said good night shamefacedly, and departed, leaving order where there had been chaos. So I kissed it, and went to bed. We met next morning as though nothing had occurred.

I scored again the following evening, through sheer luck, which sent me before bed-time to my room, in search of a handkerchief. It was only chance that showed me the pillow looking suspiciously dark as I turned off the electric light. I switched it back, and held an inspection. Pepper.

I knew a little more of my pupils now, and realized that ordinary methods did not prevail with them. Jack's room was across the passage: I carried the peppered pillow there, and carefully shook its load upon the one destined to receive his innocent head. Then I went downstairs and played accompaniments for Harry McNab, who had less voice than anyone I ever met.

The subsequent developments were all that I could have wished. The children hurried to bed, so that they might listen happily to what might follow; and the extinguishing of Jack's light was succeeded by protracted and agonized sneezing, interspersed by anxious questioning from Judy, who dashed, pyjama-clad, to investigate her ally's distress. Some of the pepper appeared to come her way as well, for presently she joined uncontrollably in the sneezing exercise. It was pleasant hearing. When it abated, smothered sounds of laughter followed.

The pair were good sportsmen. They greeted me at breakfast next day with a distinct twinkle, and—especially on Jack's part—with an access of respect that was highly gratifying. We went for a walk that day, and I improved their young minds with an eloquent discourse on the early trade from the Spice Islands. They received it meekly.

As for The Towers, in any other circumstances, to be in such a place would have been a sheer delight. The house itself was square and massive, with two jutting wings. It was built of grey stone, and crowned by a square tower, round the upper part of which ran a small balcony. Originally, I learned, the name had been The Tower House, but local usage had shortened it to The Towers, in defiance of facts. All the rooms were large and lofty, and there were wide corridors, while a very broad veranda ran round three sides of the building. It stood in a glorious garden, with two tennis-courts, beyond which stretched a deep belt of shrubbery. Then came a tree-dotted paddock, half a mile wide between the Wootong road and the house; while at the back there was but three minutes' walk to the sea.

Such a coast! Porpoise Bay, which appeared to be the special property of the McNabs, was a smooth stretch of blue water, shut in by curving headlands: wide enough for boating and sailing, but scarcely ever rough. The shore sloped gently down from low hummocks near the house, making bathing both safe and perfect. A stoutly-built jetty ran out into the water, ending in a diving-board; and there were a dressing-shed, subdivided into half a dozen cubicles, and a boat-house with room for a powerful motor-launch and a twenty-foot yacht, besides several rowing-boats.

The McNabs were as nearly amphibious as a family could be. All, even Mrs. McNab, swam and dived like the porpoises that gave their bay its name. I was thankful that Father and Colin had seen to it that I was fairly useful in the water, but I wasn't in the same class with the McNabs. It seemed to be a family tradition that each child was cast into the sea as soon as it could walk, and after that, took care of itself. Weather made no difference to them; be the morning never so rough and cold they all might be seen careering over the paddock towards the sea, clad in bathing-suits. Mrs. McNab was the only one who troubled to add to this attire, and on hot mornings she usually carried her Turkish towelling dressing-gown, a confection of striped purple-and-white, over her arm. My employer was, in the main, a severe lady; to see her long, thin legs twinkling across the back paddock filled me with mingled emotions.

Not alone in the early mornings did the McNabs bathe: at all times of the day, and even late at night, they seemed to feel the sea calling them, and forthwith fled to the shore. Visitors accompanied them or not, as they chose. I realized, early in my stay, that to shirk bathing would be a sure passport to the contempt of Judy and Jack, and accordingly I swam with a fervour little short of theirs, though I realized that I could never attain to their finished perfection in the water. They were indeed sea-urchins.

Mrs. McNab took me over most of the house on the morning after my arrival, and explained, in a vague way, what my duties were to be.

"You may have heard," she remarked, "that I am a writer."

I admitted that this was not news to me—wildly hoping that she would not cross-question me as to my acquaintance with her works. Fortunately, this did not seem to occur to her. Probably she thought—rightly—that I should not understand them.

"My work means a great deal to me," she went on. "Not from the point of money-making: I write for the few. Australia does not understand me; in America, where I hope to go next year, when Judith and Jack are at school, I have my own following. That matters little: but what I wish you to realize, Miss Earle, is, that when I am writing I must not be disturbed."

"Of course," I murmured, much awed.

"Quiet—absolute quiet—is essential to me," she went on. "My thoughts go to the winds if I am rudely interrupted by household matters. Rarely do my servants comprehend this. I had a cook who would break in upon me at critical moments to inform me that the fish had not come, or to demand whether I would have colly or cabbage prepared for dinner. Such brutal intrusions may easily destroy the effects of hours of thought."

I made sympathetic noises.

"Colly—or cabbage!" she murmured. Her hard face was suddenly dreamy. "Just as the fleeting inspiration allowed itself to be almost captured! Even the voices of my children may be destructive to my finest efforts: the ringing of a telephone bell, the sound of visitors arriving, the impact of tennis-balls against rackets—all the noises of the outer world torture my nerves in those hours when my work claims me. And yet, one cannot expect one's young people to be subdued and gentle. That would not be either right or natural. I realized long ago that the only thing for me was to withdraw."

"Yes?" I murmured.

"In most houses, to withdraw oneself is not easy," said Mrs. McNab. "Here, however, the architecture of the house has lent itself to my aid. I will show you my sanctum: the part of The Towers in which I have my real being."

We had been exploring the linen-press and pantry before the opening of this solemn subject; I had listened with a mind already striving to recollect the differences between the piles of best and second-best sheets. Now my employer turned and led the way up a narrow winding staircase that led from the kitchen regions to the upper floor. Here it grew even narrower, I followed her as it curved upward, and presently it ended on a small landing from which one door opened, screened by a heavy green curtain.

"These are the Tower rooms," Mrs. McNab said. "No one enters this door without my permission; no one, except on some very urgent matter, ascends to this landing. Here, and nowhere else, I can have the quiet which is necessary to my work."

She opened the door, using a latch-key, and waved me into a room about twelve feet square. It was thickly carpeted and very simply furnished; there were a small heavy table, a chesterfield couch and a big easy-chair, and, in a corner, a big roll-top writing desk. Low, well-filled book-cases ran round the walls, which were broken on all four sides by long and narrow windows. In another corner a tiny staircase, little more than a ladder, gave access to the upper part of the tower.

"Sit down," said Mrs. McNab. "This is the sanctum, Miss Earle, and here I am supposed to be proof against all invasion. My husband had these rooms fitted up just as I desired them: my study as you see it, and above, a tiny bedroom and a bathroom. The balcony opens from the bedroom, and on hot nights I can work there if I choose. Sometimes I retire here for days together, the housemaid placing meals at stated intervals upon the table on the landing. In hot-water plates."

"It's a lovely place," I said. "I don't wonder you love to be here alone, Mrs. McNab. It must help work wonderfully."

She gave me a smile that was almost genial.

"I see you have comprehension," she said approvingly. "But only a writer could fully understand how dear, how precious is my solitude. It is your chief duty, Miss Earle, to see that that solitude is not invaded."

"I'll do my very best," I said. I didn't know much about writing books, but any girl who had ever swotted for a Senior Public exam. could realize the peace and bliss of that silent room. There was nothing fussy in it: nothing to distract the eye. The walls, bare save for the low bookshelves, were tinted a deep cream that showed spotless against the glowing brown of the woodwork; the deep recesses of the four windows were guiltless of curtains; there were no photographs, no ornaments, no draperies. The table bore a cigarette-box of dull oak, and a bronze ash-tray, plain, like a man's: the chair before the desk was a man's heavy office-chair, made to revolve. I pictured Mrs. McNab twirling slowly in it, in search of inspiration, and I found my heart warming to her. She looked rather like a man herself as she stood by the window, tall and straight in her grey gown.

"Now and then, when I have not the wish to work, I let the housemaid come up, to clean and polish," she went on. "At all other times I keep the rooms in order myself. A little cupboard on the balcony holds brooms and mops—all my housekeeping implements. The exercise is good for me, and, as you see, there is not much to dust and arrange; my little bedroom is even more bare. A housemaid, coming daily with her battery of weapons, would be as disturbing as the cook with her ill-timed questions about vegetables for dinner. So I keep my little retreat to myself, and my work can go on unchecked."

I listened sympathetically, but more than a little afraid. It would be rather terrible if my employer went into retreat for a week or so before I knew my way about the house. The little I had seen of Beryl McNab did not make me feel inclined to turn to her for instructions. But Mrs. McNab's next words were comforting.

"Just at present I am doing only light work," she said. "A few hours each day: more, perhaps, during the night. With so many in the house I can scarcely seclude myself altogether. But I do not want to be continually troubled with household matters. I shall, of course, interview the cook each morning, to arrange the daily menu. Otherwise, Miss Earle, I shall be glad if you will endeavour to act as my buffer."

I was not very certain that I had been trained as a buffer. How did one "buff," I wondered? I tried not to look as idiotic as I felt.

"If I can, I shall be very glad to help," I mumbled. "You must tell me what to do."

She sighed.

"Ah, that is where your extreme youth will be a handicap, I fear," she said. "I should have preferred an energetic woman of about forty: and yet, Judith and Jack have such an aversion to what they call 'old frumps,' and have contrived to cause several to resign. And I liked your letter: you write a legible hand, for one thing—a rare accomplishment nowadays. I can only hope that things will go smoothly. Just try to see that the house runs as it should, and that the children do nothing especially desperate. You will need to be tactful with the servants; they resent interference, and yet, if left to themselves, everything goes wrong. Should emergencies arise, try to cope with them without disturbing me. I want my elder son and daughter to enjoy their visitors; fortunately, their main source of delight seems to be an extraordinary liking for picnics, and the basis of a successful picnic would appear to be plenty to eat. Try to get on good terms with Mrs. Winter, the cook; her last employer told me that she possessed a heart of gold, and you may be able to find it. Tact does wonders, Miss Earle."

As she delivered this encouraging address her gaze had been wandering about: now raised to the ceiling, now dwelling on the roll-top writing-desk. Towards the latter she began to edge almost as if she could not help it.

"And now, I begin to feel the desire for work," she said. "It comes upon me like a wave. Just run away, Miss Earle, and do your best. It is possible that I may not be down for luncheon." And the next moment I found myself on the landing, and heard the click of the Yale latch behind me.

I went downstairs torn between panic and a wild desire to laugh. It seemed to me that my employer was a little mad—or it might merely be a bad case of artistic temperament, a disease of which I had read, but had never before encountered in the flesh. In any case my job was likely to be no easy one. I was only eighteen; and my very soul quailed before the task of unearthing the golden heart of the cook.

In my bedroom I found Julia, the housemaid, flicking energetically with a duster. She was an Irish girl, with a broad, good-natured face. I decided that I might do worse than try to enlist her as an ally. But I was not quite sure how to begin.

I looked out of the window, seeking inspiration.

"It's pretty country, Julia," I said affably.

"For thim as likes it," said Julia. She continued to flick.

It was not encouraging. I sought in my mind for another opening, and failed to find one. So I returned to my first line of attack.

"Don't you care for the country, Julia?"

"I do not," said Julia, flicking.

"Did you come from a town?" I laboured.

"I did."

My brain felt like dough. Still, I liked Julia's face, sullen as it undoubtedly was at the moment. Her eyes looked as though, given the opportunity, they might twinkle.

"Mrs. McNab told me you came from Ireland," I ventured. "I've always heard it's such a lovely country."

"It is, then," said Julia. "Better than these big yalla paddocks."

"Don't you have big paddocks there?"

"Is it paddocks? Sure, we don't have them at all. Little green fields we do be having—always green."

"It must look different from Australia—in summer, at all events," I said. "I'd like to see it, Julia."

She glanced at me, for the first time.

"Would you, now? There's not many Australians says that: they do be pokin' fun at a person's country, as often as not. Maybe 'tis yourself is pokin' fun too?"

"Indeed, I'm not," I said hastily. "My grandmother was Irish, and though she died when I was a little girl, I can remember ever so many things that she used to tell us about Ireland. My father said she was always homesick for it."

"And you'd be that all your life, till you got back there," said Julia. She looked full at me now, and I could see the home-sickness in her eyes.

"Well, I'm homesick myself, Julia, so I can imagine how you feel," I said. She wasn't much older than I—and just then I felt very young. "My home is only a little flat in a Melbourne suburb, but it seems millions of miles away!"

"Yerra, then, I suppose it might," said Julia, half under her breath. "An' you only a shlip of a gerrl, f'r all you're that tall!"

"And I'm scared of my job, Julia," I said desperately. "I think it's a bit too big for me."

She looked at me keenly.

"Bella's afther sayin' you're only here to spy on us and interfere with us," she said. "But I dunno, now, is she right, at all?"

"Indeed, I'm not," I said hastily. "I'd simply hate to interfere. But Mrs. McNab says I am to see that the house runs smoothly, because of course she can't be disturbed when she's at work: and that is what she is paying me to do. I say, Julia—I do hope you'll help me!"

The twinkle of which I had suspected the existence came into the Irish girl's eyes.

"Indeed, then, I've been lookin' on you as me natural enemy, miss!" she said. "Quare ould stories of the other lady-companions Mrs. Winter and Bella do be havin'. Thim was the ones 'ud be pokin' their noses into everything, an' carryin' on as if they were the misthress of all the house."

"I won't do that!" I said, laughing. "I'm far too frightened."

"A rough spin was what we'd been preparin' for you," Julia said. "The lasht was a holy terror: she'd ate the face off Mrs. Winter if the grocer's order was a bit bigger than usual—an' you can't run a house like this without you'd have plenty of stores. Mrs. Winter's afther sayin' she'd not stand it again, not if she tramped the roads lookin' for work."

"But doesn't Mrs. McNab do the housekeeping?" I inquired.

"Her!" said Julia with a sniff. "Wance she gets up in them quare little rooms of hers, you'd think she was dead, if it wasn't for the amount she'd be atin'. There's the great appetite for you, miss! Me heart's broke with all the food I have to be carryin' up them stairs! She's the quare woman, entirely." She dropped her voice mysteriously. "Comin' an' goin' like a shadow she do be, at all hours of the day an' night, an' never speakin'. I dunno, now, if people must write books, why couldn't they be like other people with it all? An' the house must go like clockwork, an' no one bother her about annything! Them that wants to live in spacheless solitude has no right to get married an' have childer. 'Tis no wonder Miss Judy an' Master Jack 'ud be like wild asses of the desert!"

I had a guilty certainty that I should not be listening to these pleasant confidences. But I was learning much that would be as well for me to know, and I hadn't the heart to check Julia just as she showed signs of friendliness. So far, Dicky Atherton was the only friend I had in the house, and it was probable that Julia would be far more useful to me than he could ever be. So I murmured something encouraging, and Julia unfolded herself yet further.

" 'Tis a quare house altogether. None of them cares much for the others, only Miss Judy for Master Jack, an' he for her. Swimmin' an' divin' they do be, at all times, an' sailin' in the sea, an' gettin' upset, an' comin' in streelin' through the house drippin' wet. An' there's misfortunate sorts of sounds in the night: if 'twas in Ireland I'd say there was a ghost in it, but sure, there's no house in this country with pedigree enough to own a ghost!"

"No—we haven't many ghosts in Australia, Julia," I said, laughing. "I expect you hear the trees creaking."

Julia sniffed.

" 'Tis an unnatural creak they have, then. I don't get me sleep well, on account of me hollow tooth, an' I hear quare sounds. If it wasn't for the money I can send home to me ould mother I'd not stay in it—but the wages is good, an' they treat you well on the whole. It's no right thing when the misthress is no real misthress, but more like a shadow you'd be meetin' on the stairs. But I oughtn't to be puttin' you against it, miss, when you've your livin' to make, same as meself. It's terrible young you are, to be out in the worrld."

"I'm feeling awfully young for this job, Julia," I said. "And I'm scared enough without thinking of queer sounds, so I hope they won't come in my way. But

I do want you and Bella and Mrs. Winter to believe that I'm not an interfering person, and that I shall do my work without getting in your way any more than I can help."

"Sure, I'm ready enough to believe that same, now that I've had a quiet chat with you," replied Julia. "You've your juty to do, miss, same as meself, an' I'll help you as far as I can. Bella's not the aisiest person in the worrld to get on with: she's a trifle haughty, 'specially since she got her head shingled along of the barber in Wootong: but Mrs. Winter's all right, wance you get on the good side of her. And Bence, that's the chauffeur, is a decent quiet boy. Sure, there's none of us 'ud do annything but help to make things aisy for you, if you do the same by us."

She had gathered up her brooms and dustpan, and prepared to go. At the door she hesitated.

"And don't you be down-trodden by Miss Beryl, miss," she said. "That one's the proud girl: there's more human nature in Miss Judy's little finger than in her whole body."

"Oh, I don't think we'll quarrel, Julia," I said. "I can only do my best. At any rate, I'm very glad to think I can count on you."

She beamed on me.

"That you can, miss. An' if there's much mendin', an' I've a spare hour or two, just you hand some of it over to me: I'm not too bad with me needle. Sure, I knew Bella had made a mistake about you the minute I seen your room, left all tidy an' the bed made. I'll be off now, an' I'll tell me fine Bella that I know a lady when I see one. Anyone that's reared in the County Cork can tell when she meets wan of the ould stock!"

Father's picture seemed to smile at me as she tramped away. I think he was glad he had given me an Irish grandmother.

CHAPTER V
I WALK ABROAD AT NIGHT

HAPPILY for me, the spirit of work did not claim Mrs. McNab very violently during my first week at The Towers. There were occasional periods during which she remained in seclusion, and from the window of my room, which commanded a view of her eyrie, I sometimes saw her light burning far into the night; certainly she used to look pale and heavy-eyed in the morning. But for the greater part of each day she mingled with her family, and showed less vagueness in letting me know what were my duties. I was kept pretty busy, but there was nothing especially difficult. Already the seabathing and the country air were telling upon me: I lost my headaches, and began to sleep better, and it was glorious to feel energy coming back to me. I had visions of returning to Colin and Madge fattened out of all recognition.

Julia had evidently paved the way for me with Mrs. Winter, the cook. I found her a somewhat dour person, but by no means terrifying; she unbent considerably when she found that I did not leave the kitchen in a mess when I cut sandwiches. The last holder of my office, she told me, had always made her domain into "a dirty uproar." We exchanged notes on cookery; she taught me much about making soup, and was graciously pleased to approve of a recipe for salad that was new to her.

Bella was a harder nut to crack. She was a thoroughly up-to-date young person with an excellent opinion of herself and a firm belief that I was her natural enemy. Also, she was "work-shy," and did just as little as was possible, with a fixed determination to do nothing whatever that did not fall within the prescribed duties of a parlourmaid. We clashed occasionally: that was inevitable, though I tried hard to let the clashing be all on her side. I recalled Mrs. McNab's advice as to tact, and struggled to cultivate that excellent commodity. But I don't believe that anyone of eighteen has much tact in dealing with a bad-tempered parlourmaid of five-and-twenty. I did my best, but there were moments when I ached to throw aside tact and use more direct measures.

The house-party increased rapidly, friends of Beryl and Harry McNab arriving almost every day, until there was not a room to spare. They were a cheery, good-hearted crowd, making their own amusements, for the most part: they bathed, fished, yachted, played tennis and picnicked, and there was dancing every night, interspersed by much singing. Madge was the musical genius of our family, but I could play accompaniments rather decently, and for that reason I was constantly in request. I refused, at first, to dance, for it was quite evident that Beryl McNab preferred me to remain in the background; but there were more men than girls, and occasionally they made it impossible for me to refuse. I protested to Harry McNab, who was one of the chief offenders, but my remarks had not the slightest weight with him.

"Oh, rubbish!" he said. "Why on earth shouldn't you dance? No one expects you to work all day and all night, too—and you dance better than nearly any girl here! Don't tell me you don't like it!"

"Of course I like it," I said, with some irritation. "But I'm not here to dance, Mr. McNab, and you know that very well. Ask your sister, if you have any doubt on the matter."

"Oh—Beryl!" he said with a shrug. "Who cares what she thinks? She's not your boss, Miss Earle."

"She's the daughter of the house," I answered firmly. "And I think you would find that your mother thinks as she does."

"We'll ask her," he said. He dragged me up the long room to where his mother was sitting. Mrs. McNab never stayed downstairs for long in the evening; soon after the music was at its height she would slip away quietly to the Tower rooms and be seen no more until the morning. She greeted him with a smile that lit her rather grim face curiously. Affection was not a leading characteristic among the McNabs, but Harry was certainly first in his mother's favour.

"Miss Earle says she won't dance, Mother! Tell her it's ridiculous—three of us are standing out because we haven't got partners."

"Possibly Miss Earle does not care for dancing?"

"Yes, she does, though. Only she's got a stupid idea that you don't want her to."

"I have no objection," said his mother. "Still I do not think it would be wise for you to tire yourself, Miss Earle."

"Oh, we won't let her do that. But I'm hanged if you're going to act Cinderella all the time, Miss Earle," said Harry. "Come along—we've wasted too much of this already." He swept me out into the crowd, and I gave in more or less meekly: it wasn't difficult when every nerve in me was already beating time to the music. And Harry danced so very much better than he sang!

All the same, I never remained downstairs long after Mrs. McNab had disappeared. I had next day to consider, and my days began pretty early: besides which, I couldn't help feeling an ugly duckling amongst the other girls. My two dinner dresses were by no means up to date; I was fully aware of their deficiencies beside the dainty, exquisite frocks of which Beryl McNab and her friends seemed to have an unlimited supply. I used to breathe a sigh of relief when I escaped from the drawing-room, racing up the stairs until I gained the shelter of my own little room.

Judy and Jack were supposed to be in bed by nine o'clock. It was one of the few rules that they did not scorn, since their days were strenuous enough to make them feel sleepy early, and they had few evening occupations. They loathed dancing, and neither was ever known to read a book if it could possibly be avoided. The crowded state of the house had made it necessary for them to give up their rooms to guests: they slept on the balcony, and Judy used my room to dress, while Jack made his toilet in a bathroom. Judy was a restless sleeper, and I had formed the habit of going out to tuck her in before I went to bed.

I slipped away from the drawing-room one hot night when the dancing was fast and furious. A little breeze from the sea was beginning to blow in at my window, and I leaned out, enjoying its freshness and wondering if Colin and Madge were grilling very unpleasantly in the stuffy Prahran flat. Above my head a faint glimmer from the Tower rooms showed that Mrs. McNab was at work—one never imagined her as doing anything but writing steadily, once she had vanished to her sanctum. Sometimes she wrote on her little balcony, which was fitted with electric light: the scent of the cigarettes she continually smoked would drift down to my window on still nights.

The lower balcony that ran partly round the house ended before it reached my room, so that I had a clear view of part of the garden as well as of the track across the paddock to the sea. As I leaned out a faint sound came to me from below. Then two slight figures crossed the strip of moonlit garden, running quietly and quickly, and disappeared in the direction of the back of the house. I had been dreaming, but I came to attention with a jerk. Unquestionably, they were Judy and Jack.

I looked at my watch. Ten o'clock: and the precious pair should have been in bed an hour ago. I went down the passage and out upon the balcony to where their beds stood peacefully side by side. At first glance they appeared to be occupied by slumbrous forms; but a moment's investigation showed that a skilful arrangement of coats and pillows, humped beneath the sheets, took the places of the rightful occupants. Clearly, my charges were out upon the warpath.

I felt horribly responsible. Lawless as the two were, they were supposed to be in my care, and it seemed to my town-bred mind an unthinkable thing that two such urchins should be careering about in the dead of night. Their elaborate precautions against discovery showed that it was no excursion of a few moments. The direction of their flight was towards the sea. Possibly the McNab urge for bathing had seized them; or they would be quite equal to taking out a boat for a moonlight row. Whatever their fell designs might be, it seemed to me that I should follow them. I could not calmly go to bed, knowing that they were out of the house.

I was in anything but a gentle frame of mind while I hurriedly changed my evening frock for something more serviceable and donned a pair of tennis-shoes. Bed seemed to me a very pleasant place as I switched off my light and stole quietly down the kitchen stairs, hearing the gramophone grinding out a fox-trot in the drawing-room. I could only hope that I would find the truants soon; and that, when found, they would allow themselves to be gathered in peaceably. But I knew already that it was no easy matter to turn Judy and Jack from any set purpose.

I am a good deal of a coward in the dark; the night seemed full of ghostly sounds as I hunted up and down the dim shrubbery, hoping to find my quarry near the house. But there was no sign of them: nothing living could be seen except an old owl that flew out of a bush with a whir of wings that sent my heart into my mouth. So I set off across the paddock towards the shore.

The hummocks were fringed with low scrub, through which a dozen paths wandered. I chose one at random, following its windings until it ended in a deep, stony cleft, down which it would not be easy to scramble in the moonlight. I was about to retrace my steps, to look for an easier path to the beach, when a low giggle fell upon my ears, and looking closely, I saw Judy and Jack crouched behind a boulder below me. They had not heard me; that was clear: all their attention was focused on something beyond them. As I watched, a tall figure came from the shadow of the boat-house. I heard the scratch of a match being struck, and saw the glow as the new-comer lit a cigarette. Then the figure strolled slowly across the moonlit sand by the water, and I saw, with a start of astonishment, that it was Mrs. McNab.

She paced backwards and forwards, with her head bent, her face shadowed by one of the soft hats she always wore. She had changed her evening dress for a dark gown in which she moved like a shadow, the dull glow of her cigarette-tip the most living thing about her. There was something eerie and ghost-like in the dim form, drifting with silent steps by the gently heaving sea. I had an uneasy feeling that I was spying: that I had no right to be there. Clearly, too, it was unnecessary for me to shepherd Judy and Jack when their own mother was about. I was turning to go quietly home when another giggle came from the pair just below me, and I heard Judy's voice, discreetly lowered.

"Rotten luck!" she whispered. "No earthly chance of getting a boat out, with Mother there. Why on earth can't she stay in the Tower, without spoiling sport!"

"Let's go and give her a fright," Jack suggested. "P'raps she'll think it's one of the ghosts Julia's always talking about, and clear out!"

"Don't be an ass," counselled his sister. "She'd be awfully wild." But her words were wasted. Jack was already making his way softly down the gully.

He went more quietly than I should have imagined was possible in that cleft of shifting stones. Bending low, so that his head should not show above the edge, in case his mother glanced upwards, he crept down, and gained the beach unseen.

Mrs. McNab heard nothing. She had turned away, and was standing still, looking out to sea—doubtless seeking inspiration from the softly rippling water. I wondered would she come back presently, back to the Tower room, to write through the night; or would dawn find her still pacing by the sea. Nothing, I thought, would surprise me about my eccentric employer.

And yet, she was to surprise me—and not me alone—very much indeed.

Jack came out of the protecting gloom and stole noiselessly across the sand until he was only a dozen yards from the still figure. Then he suddenly gave a long eldritch shriek—it made even Judy jump—danced impishly for a moment, flinging about his arms and legs, and fled towards the hummocks.

Quick as he was, his mother was quicker. At his wild cry she swung round, her cigarette dropping from her fingers. She stood as if petrified for a moment. Then she gave chase. Her long legs carried her across the sand with amazing swiftness. Just as the boy gained the edge of the gully her hand fell on his shoulder and held him fast.

"You would dare to spy on me!" I heard her say, in a choked voice.

She reversed Jack with a swift movement, and then, as if he were a tiny child, she spanked him thoroughly. Jack was a strong boy and a sturdy one, and he did not take the proceeding meekly. He kicked and fought and struggled; but the grip in which he was held never slackened, and the avenging hand rose and fell with a regularity astonishing to behold. Never had I beheld a more competent spanker than Mrs. McNab. I had no special sympathy in general with Jack, but I almost ached for him.

Her arm must have been tired when the resounding blows ceased and she pitched him contemptuously on the sand. Then, without waiting to read the lecture that usually accompanies a punishment, she plunged swiftly up the gully. It is possible that she thought so thorough a spanking spoke for itself: possible, also, that she had no breath left. In any case, she did not speak. She went swiftly past me, her face lowering and angry, and her swift steps died away across the grass.

Judy had crouched low under a bush while her mother passed her. Once the avenging figure was out of sight, she sped downwards to her brother.

"My word, you caught it! I'll bet it hurt!"

"Hurt!" said Jack. He had picked himself up, and was rubbing his injuries with a comical air of bewilderment. "I'll tell the world it hurt! I'm all on fire! Great Scott! she did lay it on!" His voice took on an unwonted note of reverence. "Judy, would you have thought she had it in her?"

"I would not," said Judy. "And goodness knows, you kicked like a steer!"

"Well, I bet I don't run up against Mother again, if I can help it," Jack uttered. "I don't want another licking like that. I don't believe I'll be able to ride for a week! Judy, I tell you she held me as if I was a bit of a kitten! I'm sore, but I tell you, I'm jolly proud of Mother!"

"Well, it's a good thing that's the way it makes you feel," said Judy, regarding him with some amazement. "How about getting out that boat now? She won't come back again. She's up in the Tower room now, I bet, writing an article for the Americans on 'How I Brought Up My Sons.' Say we get the boat?"

"You don't catch me sitting in any boat to-night," returned her brother, still rubbing. "It's light walking exercise for me for a bit, and just now I think I'll take it to bed. Come along home: it must be awfully late, and there's always the chance that she might come back. I say, Judy, wasn't my yell a beauty!"

"It was," agreed his sister. "But it was a mistaken yell."

Jack nodded agreement.

"Well, you don't catch me trying to attract Mother's attention again," he said. "She leaves her mark when you do attract it. Come along, Ju: I'm off to bed."

There seemed no reason for me to show myself, when Mrs. McNab had dealt with the situation so thoroughly: I remained in my hiding-place while they clambered up the gully, a proceeding clearly fraught with pain in the case of Jack. Quite near me he paused.

"I say," he said, "we've been pretty average annoying, a good many times. I wonder why she never did that before?"

"Don't know," said Judy. "If I had a gift like that I guess I'd use it!"

"Well, I hope she won't get the habit, that's all," said Jack. They went slowly across the paddock, and I followed at a discreet distance. The light burned brightly in the Tower room as I crossed the yard. Up there Mrs. McNab would write and smoke throughout the night. For once I wanted to read the result of that particular evening's inspiration.

CHAPTER VI
I MEET GOOD FORTUNE

"WE want to get up a big boating picnic, Mother," Beryl McNab said one morning at breakfast. "Everybody is coming: the crowds from Willow Park and Karinyah, and a few people from Wootong. We're going to make a very early start, sail round some of the islands, bathe in the big diving-pools on Rocky Spit and land on Shepherd's Island for lunch. After that we'll do whatever the spirit moves us."

"Or whatever we have any energy left to do," Dicky Atherton said. "Personally, I shall lie flat on a hot patch of sand and sleep all the afternoon."

"Then you'll certainly find yourself marooned," remarked Harry. "However, if you fly a towel as a signal of distress some one will probably pick you up within a few days. And the fishing's pretty good from Shepherd's Island."

"One might be worse off," Mr. Atherton rejoined placidly. "I'm beginning to need a rest-cure, thanks to the life you people lead down here."

"We want to go on Thursday," said Beryl. "Can we have an extra-special lunch, Mother?"

"I suppose so," Mrs. McNab answered vaguely. She had been deep in thought, and it seemed an effort for her to rouse herself. It was understood in the house that the spirit of work was harassing her; she had spent most of the two previous days in the Tower rooms, and one gathered that at any moment she might be expected to go into retreat altogether. "Miss Earle, will you consult with Mrs. Winter about it? Just tell Miss Earle if there is anything in particular that you would like, Beryl."

"We're going, too!" chorused Judy and Jack.

"Oh, we don't want kids!" Beryl said. "You two are a perfect nuisance on a picnic."

"Oh, rubbish, Beryl!" Harry said. "The kids from Willow Park are coming, and they'll want mates."

Beryl shrugged her shoulders.

"Well, you can be responsible for them," she said. "But you know perfectly well, Harry, that no one ever can tell what Judy and Jack will do."

"Oh, they'll behave—won't you, kids?" said Harry easily. "I'll hammer you both if you don't. I say, Mother, I don't see how we can possibly expect Miss Earle to have a big lunch ready as early as we want to start. Why shouldn't she come too? If she had the lunch down at the boat-house about half-past twelve some of us could easily run across in the launch and pick her up."

"Good-oh!" said Jack. "I'll come back for you, Miss Earle. I can run the launch all right."

"Not by yourself, young man, thank you," said his brother. "But it would be quite easy to arrange. How about it, Mother?"

"Certainly, if Miss Earle would like to go," said Mrs. McNab, a little less dreamily. "It would be good for her. Bence could carry the baskets to the beach. You would care for the outing, Miss Earle?"

"I should like it very much, thank you," I answered, trying to keep any eagerness out of my voice. Except for bathing, I had scarcely been out of the house for some days, and the prospect of a boating picnic was alluring. Beryl had carefully refrained from making any comment, but this time it didn't worry me. There would be so many people at the picnic that it would not be difficult to keep out of her way. I heaved an inward sigh of thankfulness at the recollection of a white linen frock that would be just right, and registered a vow to find time to wash and iron it next day.

"Then that's all settled," said Harry gleefully. "I'll telephone to the other people. And just you youngsters make up your minds to behave as decently as you know how. I don't say that's much, but it may carry you through the day."

I spent a hectic day in the kitchen on Wednesday. Mrs. Winter was fighting a bad cold, and chose to resent the list of extra delicacies which Beryl had airily handed in. "One 'ud think it was a ball supper at Govinment House, instead of a picnic on a sandy island," she grumbled, and made a hundred difficulties. Beryl had disappeared; as a matter of fact, she had never appeared at all, but had sent her list by Julia; and Mrs. McNab was vaguer than ever, and had a kind of worried look that I put down to trouble over her writing. Whatever delight her work might give her when once she was shut up in her sanctum, the period while it was hatching in her brain seemed to be something like what one endures in cutting a wisdom-tooth. I felt sorry for her as she went about with her dreamy look—she was so far apart from all the cheery, happy-go-lucky house-party. At any rate, it was my job, as I recollected, to act as her buffer; and the end of it was I pretended that I had an easy day, rolled up my sleeves, and went to help in the cooking.

That cheered Mrs. Winter a good deal. She was really very seedy, with the kind of heavy head-cold that makes speech difficult and extra brain-exertion a torment: she welcomed my cooperation even more than my actual help in the work, and forgot a good many of her woes in the course of the first hour. I made oyster-patties and charlotte russe and fruit salad, and we thought out new ideas for sandwiches and cool drinks. I even managed to enlist Judy and Jack, as the best means of keeping them out of mischief; Mrs. Winter supplied them with aprons and they beat up eggs and whipped cream, and became desperately interested in my sponge-lilies and cheese-straws. "I'd be a cook myself, if I could always make things like these," Judy averred, as she sat on the table, delicately licking the cream from a sponge-lily, with a red tongue that seemed as long as an ant-eater's. "How ever do you go on cooking things like boiled mutton and steak-and-onions, Mrs. Winter, when you might make gorgeous experiments all the time?"

Mrs. Winter sniffed.

"If you had to eat theb thigs for a week, Biss Judy, you'd be botherig roud the kitched for good boiled buttod and sdeak-ad-odiods," she said severely—at which afflicted utterance the pair yelled with joy, and spent much time in devising questions that could only be answered in words containing letters impossible at the moment to the poor woman. By four o'clock we had made all the preparations that could be finished that day, and had got the dinner well under way as well. Mrs. Winter sighed with relief as I washed the kitchen table.

"I thought this bordig I'd be id by bed before dight," she said. "But I've laughed at you three so buch by cold's dearly god, I believe! Off you go, Biss Earle—you bust be tired."

"No, I'm not," I said. "I have a dress to iron yet: I'll come back and help you when I've done it. You're not to get yourself all hot over dishing-up."

" 'Deed, an' you've been enough in the kitchen for wan day," said a new voice; and Julia came in, with my rough-dry frock over her arm. "Let you run off to your tay: I'm afther bringin' this in from the line, and I'll have it ironed in two twos an' be ready to do the dishin'-up meself. Take her away, now, Miss Judy an' Master Jack. An' for pity's sake wash the two faces of ye before your Mother sees you, for there's samples on them of every blessed thing that's been cooked to-day!" Whereat Judy and Jack gripped each an arm and raced me off to my room.

I saw that they were respectable, made a hasty toilet myself, and we went out to the lawn, where afternoon tea was in full swing. A stranger was there, sitting in a basket-chair by Mrs. McNab: a spare, elderly man with keen blue eyes, at sight of whom my charges uttered a delighted yelp.

"Hallo, Dr. Firth! We've been cooking!"

"Then I won't stay to dinner, thank you," replied the stranger promptly. "Not that I believe you have; you're far too clean!"

"Oh, that's thanks to Miss Earle—she's awfully fussy about little things like that," said Judy, laughing. "This is Miss Earle, Dr. Firth. She's the worst we've had!"

"Judith!" said her mother in a voice of ice.

"I can well believe you think so, judging by your fine state of polish," said Dr. Firth, laughing. "You seem to have done wonders, Miss Earle— congratulations." He had risen to shake hands with me: I liked his firm grip and his straight glance. "Now, where are you going to sit while I get you some tea? Jack, my boy, there's a chair over there": and Jack was off like a flash to fetch it.

To be waited upon at The Towers was something new to me. I looked round nervously. But some one else had claimed Mrs. McNab's attention and every one appeared to be already supplied with tea; there was nothing for me but to do as I was bid and sit down. I did so thankfully, for I was tired enough after my day in the kitchen. Jack and Judy, already full-fed, had wandered away, and presently I was enjoying my tea, with my new friend sitting near me—our two chairs somewhat apart from the crowd.

"Now you are not to move for twenty minutes," he said, in a cool tone of command. "Doctor's orders, and therefore not to be disregarded. No, you needn't argue," as I opened my mouth. His tone was so final that I pretended that I had merely opened it to put cake into it, and he laughed.

"That's better. There are plenty of young fellows here to hand round teacups. And I want to talk to you. Mrs. McNab has been telling me that you are a doctor's daughter. Not Denis Earle's daughter, by any chance?"

"My father was Denis Earle," I said, wondering—and wondered still more at the change in his face.

"If you knew how glad I am to find you!" he said. "I knew you when you were a baby, my dear. Did Denis ever speak to you of Gerald Firth?"

"Oh—often!" I cried. "But I thought you were in England. He—he just loved you, you know!" I felt an ache in my throat; my eyes swam as I looked at his kind face.

He moved his chair so that he sheltered me from every one else.

"Drink your tea," he said quietly. "You're tired, you poor child. And I'll do the talking." He leaned forward, his voice low.

"I was in England for fifteen years—until six months ago," he said. "Then I came out hurriedly, to attend to business; my elder brother had died, leaving me his property near here. It was only just before I sailed from England that I heard that my old friend had gone; we were both bad correspondents, and not many letters passed between us. I did make inquiries about his children in Melbourne, but I couldn't get on your track: I have been intending to go down and find you, but all my brother's affairs were very tangled, and I have only just succeeded in straightening them out. It's the queerest thing that I should come across you here!"

"Oh, I'm so glad," I murmured. "It's just lovely to find some one who knew Father!"

"He and I were friends as boys and at the University," Dr. Firth said. "We took our degrees in the same year. I owe more to him than to anyone in the world—more than I could tell anyone except his own children. I was a pretty wild youngster, and I got into a horrible mess in my University days. It would have been the end of my career as a doctor, but for Denis. His help and his cool judgment pulled me through, but he went poor for three years because of it. I paid him back in money—hard enough it was to get him to take it, too. But the biggest part of it, that wasn't money, I never could repay. I'll be his debtor all my life."

He paused, and I could see that he was wrung with feeling.

"I don't know anything about it, of course," I stammered. "But Father would never have thought anything of it. You were his great friend. He often talked to us about you, and told us what mates you had been." I hesitated. "Colin is named after you: Colin Gerald Earle."

"I know," he said. "I'm rather proud of it. And where is Colin now? A full-fledged doctor, I suppose? He was a great little boy."

"He is a great boy still," I said. "He is just like Father. But he isn't a doctor, and he never will be, now. He is just a clerk in an insurance office."

"A—clerk!" he uttered. "But Denis wrote me that his whole soul was in medicine. He was to succeed your father in his practice. And you—why are you here, bear-leading these youngsters? Surely there were no money troubles?"

I told him, briefly, just how things had been. He did not say much, but it seemed to me that his face grew older.

"If I had known!" he said, when I had finished. "Denis's children! Well, I can alter one thing, at any rate: you needn't stay here as general factotum a day longer. Come over to my place, and look after me, instead: I've a huge house, and my old housekeeper will welcome you with open arms. I won't have you earning your living here."

I felt myself turn scarlet with astonishment. It was a wonderful prospect. I couldn't take it all in, but it flashed on me that it would be very soothing to meet Beryl McNab on equal terms. Then I caught sight of Mrs. McNab's face as she moved slowly across the lawn with her head bent and the look of worry plainly in her face, and I knew I couldn't do it. Father would have said it wasn't the square thing.

"It's ever so good of you, Dr. Firth," I told him, "and I'm very grateful. Some other time it would be lovely. But I couldn't throw over my job here. I don't think it would be fair to Mrs. McNab: her hands are very full, and I do believe she is beginning to depend on me."

"She could get some one else to depend upon."

"Not in the middle of the holidays. She wouldn't have taken me if she could have found some one older and more experienced. And the children are really pretty good with me—I think it's because I am young enough to play about with them now and then. They hate the elderly governess type."

"Are you working too hard?" he asked doubtfully. "You are far too thin, you know, young lady."

I told him I was by no means over-worked; there was plenty to do, but nothing really difficult. He was not satisfied: that was clear. He asked me a great many questions, and finally repeated that Mrs. McNab should be asked to find some one to replace me.

We were supposed to be an obstinate family, and I may have a certain share of the quality. At any rate, I shook my head.

"Please don't ask me, Dr. Firth, for I hate saying 'No' to your kindness. But I've undertaken a responsibility, and I don't feel that I can drop it. You know, Father always taught us that it was an unpardonable thing to let anyone down."

He looked at me keenly.

"Yes, you're like Denis," he said. "Well, I won't try to persuade you against your own judgment. But I warn you, I shall keep an eye upon you, and if I see that you are getting fagged, I shall write to Colin and take the law into my own hands. Give me his address, please"—he wrote it down—"and promise that you will tell me if I can help you in any difficulty. I know the McNabs pretty well."

I promised that readily enough.

"But I don't think there will be real difficulties," I said. "I am beginning to feel that I can hold down my job, and I like the children. And it will all seem so different, now that I know I have a friend close by. I shan't be lonesome any more."

"I'm glad you feel like that about it," he said. "And now, I suppose, I had better find my hostess: every one seems to have gone over to the tennis-courts." He made me go with him, and we looked for Mrs. McNab, who was sitting alone, knitting, under a big jacaranda.

"You have had a long talk," she said, her voice rather cold.

"We have," Dr. Firth said cheerfully. "I have found an old friend, Mrs. McNab: I knew this young lady in her cradle. Her father was my greatest friend. It has been a very great pleasure to discover one of his children."

"That is very nice," said Mrs. McNab absently. "Won't you sit down? Dr. Firth, have you heard anything of the robbery last night? Or is it only a rumour?"

"No rumour, worse luck. Some mean scoundrel broke into the Parkers' cottage—you know, those two old maiden sisters who live on the outskirts of Wootong: they used to keep a little fancy shop, but they retired last year. Last night they went to choir-practice, leaving their place locked up, as usual. Some one managed to open the kitchen window and climb in, and when they came home they found their writing-table ransacked."

Mrs. McNab leaned forward, looking anxious.

"Did they—was there much taken?"

"The thief was evidently looking for money only. Unfortunately, the old ladies had money in the house: a foolish habit of theirs. The writing-table drawers had flimsy modern locks, easily enough picked by anyone with a little skill in that direction. The rascal got away with five-and-twenty pounds."

"How dreadful!" Mrs. McNab said. "I am so sorry for them. And—the police? are they looking for the thief?"

Dr. Firth shrugged his shoulders.

"Oh, of course. But the Wootong policemen aren't a very brilliant pair, and the man left no trace, they say. It is so easy, nowadays, to get away with the proceeds of a robbery; a motorcar or motor-cycle lands a thief forty miles away in an hour. And the Parkers' cottage is on the main road, where cars pass every few minutes. I don't suppose the poor old ladies have much chance of seeing their money again. It is a heavy loss for them: they have very little to live on, and the elder sister is not strong."

"Poor old things!" Mrs. McNab said, in a troubled tone. "It was a very mean robbery."

"It was; and it looks as though the thief knew something of their circumstances. One would not expect a little cottage like that to be burgled;

the ordinary thief would hardly expect to get enough to make his risk and trouble worth while. Some people are saying that the burglar is not far off. It appears that Henessy, of the hotel, lost some money last week; some one had helped himself from the till. Henessy had been in and out of the bar a good deal, and a great many people had been there during the day; he felt that he had no clue, so he held his tongue at the time. But he told the constable about it this morning."

"But that is very worrying to the whole neighbourhood," said Mrs. McNab anxiously. "You should be careful, Dr. Firth: your house is lonely, and you have so many beautiful things in it."

"Oh, they're well enough secured, I fancy," he said. "My brother had very special locks for all his cabinets of curiosities. All the same, I admit that I think there is too much there for prudence. I have none of the collector's fever, as my brother had, and a good many of his treasures mean very little to me, valuable as they are. They would not be much use to the average burglar, either."

"Oh, but think!" Mrs. McNab urged, leaning forward. "The jewels set in those barbaric ornaments—they would be easily removed. I don't think you should run the risk."

"Well, yes, I suppose the jewels would make decent plunder," Dr. Firth admitted. "To tell you the truth, Mrs. McNab, I don't seem to have had time to learn my brother's collections yet: there are ever so many things of which I have only a hazy notion. They are all listed, of course, and I had an expert down to value them, in connection with Michael's estate; but since then they have been locked away." He looked almost apologetic as he spoke. "I'm pretty busy, you know: there has been so much business to see to, and so much writing to England—I left at a moment's notice when the news of Michael's death came. And the local people won't believe that I am not a practising physician: they come to me whenever Dr. Harkness is not to be found in Wootong. I tell them it's their own risk, considering that I haven't practised my profession for fifteen years. But one can't refuse them. So my time is sadly cut to waste. But for that I should have found out Miss Earle and her brother and sister long ago: and then, I doubt if you'd have had Miss Earle here, for I should have wanted her myself."

To my astonishment, Mrs. McNab looked genuinely concerned.

"You do not want to take her away, I hope?"

I shot him a warning glance, and he laughed as he answered the quick question.

"I don't imagine that she would come if I suggested it," he said lightly. "But don't let her over-do it, Mrs. McNab: she is not as strong as she might be. I mean to exercise my rights as an old family friend and keep a sharp eye upon her."

"Oh!" said my employer. "Quite so. By all means, Dr. Firth. But I trust that we are not overworking Miss Earle. Though indeed," she added, apparently recollecting something, "I was much horrified, on going to the kitchen just now, to see how my cook is, to be shown all the cookery you have done to-day. Piles of dainties. But quite unusual, I assure you, Dr. Firth."

"Quite," I said, laughing. "I haven't gone in for such a baking orgy since I left my cookery class. It was really great fun, Mrs. McNab, and Judy and Jack enjoyed it, too. Please don't worry about me. I am really much stronger than when I first came here."

"I am very glad to hear you say so," Mrs. McNab said. "Indeed, Dr. Firth, I should be sadly lost without Miss Earle. For one so young she has surprising tact in dealing with cooks and children!" At which I turned a brilliant red, and Dr. Firth laughed and said good-bye. I walked with him to the gate, where his car stood. Just as he started the engine, Judy and Jack came tearing up.

"When are we to come over to see you? You said we were to come one day in the holidays!"

"So you are. Miss Earle, too, if she will: I'll telephone and fix a day. And look here, you two: I knew Miss Earle when she was much younger than either of you, and she is my charge. Just you behave decently to her, or you needn't expect to be friends with me." He nodded over the wheel at them, and was gone.

Judy and Jack looked at each other.

"Well, I like that!" uttered Jack. "He was about the only one in the country that didn't jaw at us, and now he's begun!"

"And there wasn't any need to jaw, either," added his sister. "For we do treat you quite beautifully, don't we, Miss Earle?"

"Quite," I told them. "We have established friendly relations."

"I'm hanged if I'm friendly with most of my relations," said Jack. "They're a moulty lot: always on the jump for what a fellow's going to do next. But you're sensible, Miss Earle."

"Yes," said Judy. "You don't expect us to behave like angels every bit of our time."

"I do not—and isn't it a good thing?" said I. "But I would be really glad if you would try to check your queer desire to put things into people's beds. I really didn't mind the Jew-lizard you put into mine, because I have met Jew-lizards before, and also because I found him before I got into bed. But Miss Vaughan was quite peevish about the frog she found in hers last night."

"He was a gorgeous green one!" said Judy soulfully. "Do tell us what she said, dear Miss Earle!"

"I will not: there was too much of it for me to remember. But you might bear in mind that I reap the harvest when you sow frogs. If Dr. Firth heard——"

"Oh, he mustn't!" Judy cried. "Miss Earle, he's got the jolliest place ever. It belonged to old Mr. Michael Firth, who was a perfect Jew and hated every one, so, of course, no one went there. Then he kindly died, so this brother inherited it, and he's a dear. The house is just full of queer things that old Mr. Firth collected. He never would let anyone look at them, except people as snuffy as himself, but Dr. Firth is going to show us everything. I'm so glad he's going to let you come too!"

I went to my room that night, tired enough, but with a heart lighter than it had been since my arrival at The Towers. Mrs. Winter had beamed upon me after dinner, and had forbidden me to come near the kitchen next morning, remarking that if she could not pack a few baskets her name was not Susad Widter. Julia had left my white frock on a hanger in my wardrobe, ironed to a glossy smoothness of perfection that was heartsome to see; and even Bella had unbent from her haughty pedestal to hope that the weather to-morrow might be fine. I had not again encountered Mrs. McNab, who had disappeared directly after dinner into her upper fastness: but her words in the garden with Dr. Firth had been reassuring. Judy and Jack were friendly— even roughly affectionate. It really seemed that my holiday job might be a success.

And, best of all, I had found an old friend. A good many of our friends had vanished after we fell on evil times. No one had been actively unpleasant; we simply felt that we were outside the circle, and we had made up our minds, rather bitterly, that money was the only thing that counted. To meet Dr. Firth, with his warm memories of Father, had helped me wonderfully, even though I had not felt able to do as he wished in leaving The Towers. It was delightful to think that we were to have his friendship after I had gone back to Prahran. Now—what a jolly letter I could write to Colin and Madge! I could not wait a moment to begin: I found writing materials hurriedly, and in a moment my pen was fairly flying over the paper.

It was late when I finished. My eyes were aching, and I switched off the light and leaned out of the window. Every one seemed to have gone to bed: the house was very still, and the scent of a great bush of bouvardia under my window came up to me in a wave. I stayed there dreaming, until I began to feel cold, and found myself yawning.

Just as I turned to undress and go to bed a faint sound below caught my ear. I held my breath to listen. Clearly there was some one below: the muffled, stealthy steps were unmistakable. The memory of the Wootong burglar flashed upon me. Was the thief about to try his luck at The Towers?

As I listened, the soft movements passed from the path beneath my window, and seemed to come from the direction of the yard. I heard a faint crunch that could only be the gravel at the back. There, I knew, everything was locked up—Mrs. Winter had a pious horror of unfastened doors and windows, and saw that all were secure every night before she went to her room. I resolved to reconnoitre a little farther before alarming the house. In a moment I was running softly down the back staircase.

Half-way down, a sudden sound brought me to a standstill, trembling. Some one had come in and had closed a door, very gently. In a moment stealthy steps were mounting the stairs towards me.

There was no time to get back to my room: quiet as the steps were, they were swift—whoever was coming was almost on me. The scream which all proper young persons should be able to produce refused to come from my lips; my feet would not move. I put out my hand to the wall to steady myself, shrinking away, and my fingers encountered an electric light switch. Almost without knowing what I did, I turned it on.

The light, magically transforming the black darkness, shone full on Mrs. McNab, coming up the stairs in her dark day gown and soft hat. She might have been out for a morning walk. But the glimpse I had of her face under the brim of the hat staggered me, so white was it and so haggard.

"I beg your pardon, Mrs. McNab!" I stammered. "I thought you were a burglar!"

She had started violently when the light flashed out—started almost as though she would run away. Then she came on swiftly, and brushed rudely past me, without a word or glance. I stood staring after her, but she did not turn. Her quick strides took her beyond the landing: I heard her feet on the upper staircase, and then the click of her door as it shut.

I made my way upstairs, still trembling. Within the shelter of my room I collapsed on my bed, thankful for its support.

"Well!" I uttered. "Literary genius may make you do queer things, Mrs. McNab, but it needn't give you the manners of a jungle pig!"

CHAPTER VII
I FIND SHEPHERD'S ISLAND

MY queer encounter with my employer did not, luckily, hinder my sleep: I went to bed, and knew nothing more until Julia brought me a cup of tea at seven o'clock. It was long after my usual time for rising, and I felt almost panicky as I glanced at my watch.

"Oh, Julia, I'm awfully late!" I said ruefully. "Why didn't you call me before?"

"Is it me to be callin' you?" was Julia's inquiry. "Sure, it's glad I am to see you taking a bit of a rest. I dunno why would you always want to be leppin' from your bed before annywan in the house—you, that's afther tellin' me you want to get fat!"

"And so I do," I said. "But it makes all the day easier if I have a good start. Julia, this tea is heavenly!"

"Drink it slow and aisy, then," said Julia. "No need to gulp it as if you were emptyin' a cup for a wager. And you'll do no more worrk than you can't help doin' this fine day, miss: remember 'tis a picnic you have before you, and the finest day ever I seen to enjoy it in. There's no sense in goin' out worrn to the bone with slaving for them as doesn't notice it."

"Don't you believe it, Julia," I told her, laughing. "Mrs. McNab as good as said yesterday that she couldn't do without me!"

"Yerra, I knew that," said Julia with great calmness. "What I didn't know was that she'd woke up enough to find it out! Well, good luck to the poor woman—it seems there's sense comin' to her in her ould age!"

"Why, she isn't old at all," I said. "I don't think she is much over forty—she told me she had married when she was just out of the schoolroom."

"That one'll never see youth again, no matther how ould she may be," Julia said. "The only signs of youth ye'd see on her is when she do be stridin' across the paddock in her bathin' clothes; all other times she looks as ould as McFadden's pig, with the look of trouble she have on her. I dunno why wouldn't she take life aisy instead of writin' all day an' all night as well: an' they say there's no end to her riches. 'Tisn't meself 'ud worrk if I had them."

"How is Mrs. Winter?" I asked, to change the subject. I knew I should not listen to Julia's opinions of her mistress, but I had a guilty joy in doing so, nevertheless.

"Her spache is no aisier to the poor woman, but her spirits is good. I rubbed her shesht for her last night till I nearly brought the blood, an' then I gave her a good hot glass of lemon an' other things to comfort her—roarin' at me she was to stop long before I'd finished. She have flannin on it to-day, she's afther tellin' me, with oil on it, to soothe the rawness. There's nothin' like a good rub to get rid of a cold an' keep it from settlin' on the shesht. Don't be worryin' yourself about her; she told me to tell you she felt gay as a lark!"

"She has great endurance," I said solemnly.

Julia twinkled.

"I dunno would you have said so if you'd heard her last night," she said with a grin. " 'Lave me,' says she, 'while I have anny skin left on me body!' 'I will not lave you,' I says, 'till I have you in a nice, plisant glow!' 'Tis the grand muscle I have for rubbin', along of polishin' the floors, an' I med good use of it on her. She'll be the betther of it this manny a day."

"Will you rub me, Julia, if I get a cold?" I asked, as well as I could for laughter.

"I will that same."

"Then I won't get one," I said firmly. "Julia, the tea was lovely, and I could talk to you for a week—but I must get up. I wish it was time for me to put on my white frock, for it was never ironed so beautifully in its life!"

The Irish girl beamed.

"Did you like it? I'm glad. Me ould mother taught us ironin', back in Skibbereen; she'd have broke our legs from under us if we'd lef' so much as a crease in the tail of a shirt. There'll be no frock among all them fine young ladies at the picnic lookin' betther than yours, miss. Just you take it aisy, now, an' don't get tired; I'll keep me eye on Bella an' see she don't put down fish-knives for the quality to use for their porridge!" She picked up my cup and departed.

I found myself singing as I dressed. Julia always had an uplifting effect upon me: and with all her quaint friendliness there was never any lack of respect. Occasionally I had daydreams, in which Colin had won Tattersall's sweep or found a gold-mine, so that we swam in amazing wealth; and always in my dreams we transferred Julia from The Towers to grace our newly acquired marble halls. Julia herself was much uplifted at the prospect, rather dismaying me by a childlike belief that some day the vision would become reality. I knew how little chance there was of that; still—where would one be without even hopeless dreams?

I greeted Mrs. McNab at breakfast in some trepidation, the memory of the tragic meeting of the previous night weighing upon me. To my relief, she had evidently decided to ignore it: she gave me a pleasant "good morning," and actually inquired whether I had slept well—a courtesy somewhat marred by the fact that she did not listen to my reply. That, however, was nothing unusual with Mrs. McNab: her attention rarely lasted beyond one's first speech. It used to give one the rather embarrassing feeling of talking into a telephone disconnected at the other end.

The house-party trooped off as soon as breakfast was over, accompanied by Judy and Jack, whose spotless condition would, I felt grimly certain, not endure beyond the first landing-place. Harry McNab lingered to give me final instructions.

"I've told Bence to be on hand when he's wanted, in case Mother forgets," he said. "He's to carry everything down to the boat-house—don't you go making a baggage-mule of yourself, Miss Earle. Will you be down about half-past twelve? I can't be quite certain of being there for you on time, but I promise I won't keep you waiting long. We'll all have enormous appetites, so I hope you and Mother Winter have fixed up heaps of lunch, and that it isn't all Beryl's kickshaws! I'll want dozens of sandwiches—big, thick ones, with the crust left on!"

"I'll make you up a special package," I told him. "But don't let your sister see them, or I'll be eternally disgraced."

"Great Scott, all the other fellows will want them, too!" he laughed. "Make us plenty, and we'll get behind a rock and devour them where Beryl can't see them. Beryl's far too refined for the sort of picnic we're going to have to-day!"

I braved Mrs. Winter's wrath by going to the kitchen to cut sandwiches of a size remarkable enough to satisfy the hungriest; but this light exercise was the only work I was permitted to do that morning, for Julia and the cook effectually blocked any attempts I made to justify my position as a paid helper. Finally, I gave up trying to find work, and went off to my room, where I read *Greenmantle* and spent a morning of utter peace and enjoyment, until it was time to dress. Julia was waiting for me when I came downstairs, and nodded approval of my frock.

" 'Tis aisy seen that bit of linen came out of Ireland," she said. "It do hang lovely, miss: an' that big black hat wit' one rose in it is just what it wants. You wouldn't mind, now, comin' out by way of the kitchen, an' lettin' Mrs. Winter see you?"

"I meant to," I said.

Their cheery good-byes rang pleasantly in my ears as I strolled down to the shore. Bence had already taken the lunch. He met me near the edge of the hummocks: a tall young fellow, with a quiet manner, and a dark, good-looking face.

"Everything is stacked at the end of the jetty, miss," he said. "I see Mr. Harry comin' across in the launch: he'll be there in a few minutes. It's a great day for a picnic."

"Thank you, Bence: yes, it is a perfect day," I answered. And, indeed, it was perfection; not too hot, yet hot enough to make bathing glorious; a blue sea, flecked here and there with a little white cap, and air so clear that the islands were golden against the blue. Seagulls and terns strutted on the wet sand by the water: overhead, gannets wheeled and hovered, now and then plunging downwards, throwing high the spray as they disappeared in quest of darting fish. Across the bay the launch came shooting swiftly: Harry McNab perched forward, with a rope ready, while, as they drew nearer, I could see the flushed faces of Judy and Jack, and shrill, triumphant cries greeted me:

"We ran her all by ourselves, Miss Earle! Harry didn't do a thing! Jack ran the engine, and I steered——"

"And you'd better stop talking, or you'll scrape half her paint off on the side of the jetty," quoth Harry; to which Judy's only answer was a derisive snort. She brought the launch deftly alongside, and I caught the rope round a bollard. Harry sprang out, and in a few moments the baskets were stowed away, and we shoved off.

"The kids really managed fairly well," said Harry, in the half-contemptuous tone of an elder brother. "They were mad keen to come over for you alone, but I didn't see much point in that."

"Pif—we didn't need you!" said Judy loftily. "Bence has been teaching us for ever so long; I bet we know as much about the engine as you do, Mr. Harry, so there!"

"Bence says I'd make a jolly good mechanic," stated Jack, looking up from the engine with a happy face, to which a large streak of oil lent pleasing variety.

"When you grow up I expect you might," Harry jibed. "Anyhow, it's not very difficult. Ever run a launch, Miss Earle?"

I nodded.

"Yes—though I'm not an expert. But I like anything to do with an engine."

"You're a queer girl," said Harry reflectively. "Most Melbourne girls don't know a thing about the country, or engines, or anything of that kind, but you're different. You weren't even scared of the bull the other day!"

"That's all you know," I answered. "I was horribly scared, but I knew it wouldn't do to let the old bull see it. You see, though we were brought up in Melbourne, Father took us to the country every summer: we generally hired a launch and camped out. Father didn't believe in any of us being unable to manage the launch, if necessary, so we all had to serve an apprenticeship. And I happen to like engines, so I picked up a good bit. Father was a very stern camper!"

"How d'you mean, stern?" demanded Jack.

"Well, he believed in a camp being run properly. Everything had to be ship-shape, and he made us do things really well, from digging storm-water drains round the tents to burying and burning the rubbish every day. Father used fairly to snort when he spoke of people who leave greasy papers and tins lying about in the bush, to say nothing of egg-shells and orange-peel. We had to take it in turns to be cook and camp-manager, and he held a daily inspection of everything, from the rolling of the blankets to the washing of the frying-pan."

"I say—that's making camping into a job of hard work!" uttered Harry.

"No, it wasn't—not a bit. It only made us camp-proud, and I can tell you, our camp was worth looking at. We enjoyed it ever so much more, and we had hardly any bother with flies and ants. We had heaps of fun; Father was the best mate that ever lived. Ship-shape camping is very easy when every one knows his job and sticks to it. And it makes a big difference when you come back tired and hungry after a long day, to find firewood and water all ready, and everything clean."

"There's something in that," Harry admitted. "Six of us were camping last Christmas; we used to shoot off after breakfast, leaving things anyhow, and the greasy plates were pretty beastly at night: and we were eaten alive with flies and creepy things. Then rain came, and we were flooded out. It wasn't a whole heap jolly. I'll try your idea of a drain next time, Miss Earle."

We had rounded the western headland of Porpoise Bay and were out in open water. Before us was a long stretch of blue, dotted with a dozen little islands—some mere heaps of rounded granite boulders, their sides washed smooth by the waves, others clothed with trees and undergrowth. The largest of these was a couple of miles ahead. It was a long, narrow island, densely wooded at one end, and with smooth green slopes running down to the water's edge. A little building showed not far from the beach, half hidden by the trees.

"That's Shepherd's Island," Harry nodded.

"Is there a shepherd there? Surely there are no sheep?"

"There have been a good many sheep there, occasionally. There's always grass on the Island—a little creek runs through it, fed from a spring—and the feed is quite good. In very dry seasons some of the farmers used to ferry their sheep across, and they did very well there. Then some bright spirits realized that it was an easy place to get mutton, and the sheep began to disappear. That annoyed the owners, so they clubbed together and put a man out there to watch the flock: they built him a stone hut, and used to take him supplies every week. But the seasons have been so good for some years that there has been no need to send sheep across, so the old hut hasn't been used."

"What a lonely place for a man to live in!" I commented.

"Oh, it wasn't too bad. The Island is only a mile in a direct line from the shore, and some of the fishing-boats used to look him up from time to time, besides the weekly supply-boat. And there was always the chance of a scrap with sheep-stealers; the shepherds used to be provided with a gun, though I think only one man ever used it—and then he killed a sheep by mistake! There's good fishing from the rocks at the far end, too. I don't fancy a fellow would be too badly off there," Harry ended. "I think Mother might do worse than go and camp there with her writing: an island is just about what she wants, when a book is worrying her!"

That seemed to me a rather brilliant idea, and I was wondering how it would appear to Mrs. McNab when we drew near to Shepherd's Island. A shelf of rock at the edge of a deep, tiny bay made a natural landing-place; already two other launches were secured there, their mooring-ropes tied to trees. We ran in gently, Judy at the helm. Several people, Dicky Atherton among them, were waiting for us.

"Thought you were never coming," he called out. "We're all stiff with hunger!"

"You're very lucky to get us at all," Harry retorted. "Catch the rope, Dick. I hope you've got the billy boiling."

"It ought to be, if it isn't. Hallo, Miss Earle—you're the coolest-looking person on this island! We're all hot and hungry and sunburnt, but we've had a great time." He helped me ashore and introduced me to several people whom I had not seen before. The launch was unloaded, and we set off up the smooth grassy slope to where the main body of the picnickers could be seen gathered under a shady tree. To the left the smoke of their fire drifted lazily upward.

Beryl McNab was cool and aloof, and did not attempt to make me known to any of the strangers. But some of the other girls were kinder, and among the Wootong contingent I discovered an old school-chum, and we fell on each other's necks with joy: I had not seen Vera Curthois for years, but she was one of those to whom lack of money makes no difference. She introduced me to the people with whom she was staying: merry, friendly girls and boys.

Harry and Dicky Atherton superintended lunch, not permitting me to do anything; and presently I seemed to know every one, and managed to forget that I was a kind of housekeeper and paid buffer to Mrs. McNab. It was very refreshing to be simply Doris Earle once more: I enjoyed every minute of the long, cheery luncheon.

We explored the island after everything was packed up and we had rested for awhile under the trees. The shepherd's cottage was not much to see; a one-roomed hut built of slabs and heavy stones, joined by a kind of rough mortar. Cobwebs festooned it, and birds had nested in the crevices, but it was still water-tight, though the door sagged limply on one hinge. I fancied that Mrs. McNab would prefer her snug retreat in the Tower rooms. It was easy, looking at it, to picture the lonely shepherd who had waited in the darkness, his gun across his knees, for the sound of oars grating in rowlocks as the sheep-stealers' boats drew near. A man might well get jumpy enough to fire into the gloom and kill his own sheep.

"It's a big island, but the place where we landed is the only bit of the shore that's safe to bring a boat alongside," said Harry. "Even there, you want to be careful; there are sunken rocks everywhere. Most of the visitors funk it, though of course it's nothing when once you know the way. The local people have rather exaggerated the difficulties, to discourage boating parties from landing here when there were sheep: there are plenty of city gentlemen, out for the first time with a rifle, who would think it rather sporting to fire at a stray sheep on these hills."

"Sort of chaps who pot black swan and seagulls," said Jack with disgust.

"Yes; the coast swarms with them in the holidays. However, they generally let Shepherd's Island alone, thank goodness!"

"But you can land near Smugglers' Cave," said Judy.

"Oh yes—if you know the entrance. But it's so masked with rocks that no one would dream of putting in there who wasn't thoroughly familiar with the place. It was rather lucky for the shepherds who had to camp here that there is only one good landing: if they had had to watch all the shore at night their job would have been a fairly tough one. As it was, they could keep a look-out from the door of the hut."

"This is a stuffy old place!" Judy said contemptuously. "Let's go down to the other end of the Island: I want to show you the Smugglers' Cave, Miss Earle."

"Were there smugglers?" I asked.

"Never a smuggler!" Harry McNab answered, laughing. "But there's a cave of sorts, and of course it had to have a name."

"All the best caves have smugglers," Vera smiled. "Come and we'll explore it, Doris."

We went along the shore of the Island. The sandy beach soon gave place to rocks, at first low and scattered, but presently rugged and steep, with masses of rounded boulders flung hither and thither. The outgoing tide had left innumerable pools among them, fringed with red and bronze seaweed and big crimson anemones. We lingered among them until eldritch screams from Judy smote upon our ears, and we beheld her dancing on a huge flat-topped rock and calling to us to hurry.

I was used to wild outcries on the part of Judy and Jack, but on this occasion there seemed unusual urgency in the call, and I hurried accordingly.

"I thought you were never coming!" she greeted me. "Jack's stuck in a rock, and we can't get him out. I don't believe anything ever will, unless they use dynamite, and then they'll dynamite him too!"

"But how exciting!" laughed Vera. "Lead us to the painful scene, Judy, won't you?"—and Judy suddenly turned upon her, her face aflame.

"You haven't got anything to laugh at!" she flung at her. "If it was your brother stuck you wouldn't think it was so jolly funny. I suppose you think it's a joke for a little kid to be hurt!"

"Steady, Judy!" I said.

"Well, she laughed!" said Judy furiously.

"I wouldn't have laughed, Judy dear, if I had known he was hurt," Vera said contritely. "Come on, and we'll see if we can't get him out."

We found the prisoner with his feet tightly wedged between two rocks, in a deep cleft. He had slipped from above, so that both feet were jammed: and since it was impossible for him to get any purchase on the water-worn granite, he was perfectly helpless. Three youngsters of his own age, lying flat on the rock above the cleft, were hauling at his arms, with no result whatever, except to cause him a considerable amount of pain. His rosy face was very near tears as he looked up at us.

"I thought a grown-up would never get here!" he said dolefully. "What am I going to do, Miss Earle? I can't move an inch!"

"We'll get you out, Jack, old man," I said. "Don't struggle, or you may be more jammed than ever."

Vera and I examined the situation, while the children stood about us with anxious faces. We tried to lift him, but it was clear from the first that it was beyond our strength. As I lay face downwards above him a dull boom and a splash sounded behind me, and a swirl of green water flowed into the cleft.

"Tide's coming in," said Jack between his teeth. "That's the third wave, and each has been a bit higher. It comes up from somewhere underneath me. Could you hurry a bit, Miss Earle?"

"Judy," I said quickly, "run for some of the men—your brother and Mr. Atherton, if you can see them, but any of the men will do. You others scatter and look for any long pieces of timber you can find. Stay with him, Vera— I'm going to the boats for rope."

I used to be a pretty good runner at school, when I captained the hockey team, but I don't think I ever ran as I did along that horrible island. It seemed miles long; when I had to leave the grass the sand held my feet back, and I ploughed through it in ungainly bounds. I saw no one: all the others were on the western shore, where one of the boys had landed a big fish—so big that every one had become excited and had insisted on trying to fish too. Judy's search was fruitless for a time: a fact of which I was luckily unaware, as I raced to the launches, lying lonely and quiet by the rocky shelf. I seized a coil of the stoutest rope I could see, and fled back again. Every wave breaking lazily on the beach below me, struck new terror into my heart. I knew how quickly the tide turned on that coast: how swiftly such a cleft as the one in which Jack was trapped would fill with water, drawn up into it by suction from the rock-spaces beneath him. His set little face swam before my eyes, as I ran, lending new strength to my lagging feet: the square, dirty boy-face, with the honest eyes. I think I tried to pray, only no words would come.

Others were running, too, as I neared the rocks again: I saw Dicky Atherton and Harry, and a big young man in a gorgeous sweater, whose colours had offended my eye at lunch—I welcomed it now, remembering how big and strong he was. He carried a long pole: a young tree-trunk, lopped for some purpose, and washed over from the mainland: even laden as he was, he ran with the athlete's long, easy strides. Panting, I reached the cleft again, brushing through the group of scared children.

The water was waist-deep round Jack now, and as I came in sight of his face a wave washed into the cleft, sending a hurrying rush of water to his shoulders. And even so, he gave me a little smile.

"Golly, you must have run, Miss Earle!" he said.

"Rope!" said a voice at my shoulder. "Oh, by Jove, that's good!" Dicky Atherton snatched the coil from my hands and flung himself into the cleft, knotting it swiftly under the boy's arms.

"Don't you get caught too, Dicky," warned Jack.

"Don't you worry, old man—my feet are too big," Dicky said, laughing. I wondered how he could laugh at such a moment; and wondered the more when I saw how his face had whitened under its tan. But Jack grinned back.

Dicky Atherton sprang up to the top again, gathering the rope until it was taut. The big young man had thrust his pole deep into the cleft near Jack: on the other side, Harry had done the same with a long fence-rail that some one had found on the shore. They glanced at each other.

"Ready—all together!" said Harry breathlessly. "Pull, Dicky!"

They bent on their levers, thrusting them deeper into the swirling water, while Dicky leaned back against the rope. I saw Jack set his lips as it tightened. For a moment nothing gave; and then the dry fence-rail split and shivered under the strain, and Harry went staggering back with a little gasp of despair. There was a kind of shudder through the group round the rock. Then the good green timber found its grip and held, and as the big man flung his weight on it, the rock moved and Jack's shoulders came up. Harry sprang to add his strength to the pull: together he and Dicky drew the little prisoner up, and in a moment he was safe upon the top.

Beryl McNab broke into noisy crying.

"Oh, I thought it was all over when that rail broke!" she sobbed.

"Not much!" said Jack. He was very white, and his voice shook, but his eyes twinkled still. He put out a hand to Judy, who had neither moved nor spoken. She went on her knees beside him, holding the grubby little hand in a close grip.

"Hurt much, old Jack?" she asked with stiff lips.

"I feel as if I was all skinned with the rope," Jack said, sitting up and rubbing himself. "Oh, and, by Jove, look at my legs! I've lost my sand-shoes!"

He had lost more than sand-shoes. Not only had they been pulled off, but his feet and ankles were almost skinned, with deep cuts and grazes from which the blood was now pouring.

"Golly, and I never felt a thing!" said Jack, much interested. "Why, I'm like a skinned rabbit! Well, I guess I'll keep out of that sort of hole after this. Jolly lucky for me there were so many people about, wasn't it?"

"Jolly lucky we had that rope," said the big man gravely. "Look at that beastly place now."

The cleft was almost full of water that moved to and fro with a dull surge. The rescue had been only just in time. I think we all shuddered, looking into the green depths. Then, since shuddering was not much use, and the rock where we stood would soon be covered with water, I made a collection of handkerchiefs and bound up Jack's wounds, after soaking them in water. The men proposed to carry him, but he scorned the idea, declaring himself perfectly well able to walk.

"I'll paddle round to the launch and get into my bathers," he said, standing up and shaking himself, his wet clothes clinging limply to his little body. "Come along, Ju." He went off, limping, but erect, Judy's arm round his shoulders. I think, of the two, I was more sorry for Judy.

Harry and I followed, to examine his other wounds—Beryl being apparently too unnerved to do anything but sit on a rock in a becoming attitude and bewail what might have been. We found that the rope had cut through his thin shirt, marking him in an angry circle: it was sore enough, but we could only be thankful that it was no worse. Jack himself asked for no consolation.

"I'm all right," he said sturdily. "It was all my own fault, anyhow. You ought to make Miss Earle have a cup of tea, Harry; she ran all the way to the launch and back for the rope, and she must be tired."

"That's a good idea, young 'un," said Harry. "Come along, Miss Earle: you sit under a tree, and I'll boil the billy."

The others came straggling back, and we had tea; and then, since Jack was peacefully fishing from a rock in his bathing suit, and vigorously protested against being taken home, we left him in Judy's care and strolled back to see the Smugglers' Cave.

As Harry had said, it was not much of a cave. It was wide and shallow, with a tiny compartment opening off it—a sub-cave, Vera called it. Both were floored with smooth dry sand. The most interesting thing about the place was the sea in front of the opening. The rocks ran far out into the water all along that part of the Island shore; but just before the cave there were none, and instead there stretched a little calm bay, almost circled by the high rocks.

"That is really what gave the place its name," Harry said. "Some one started the yarn that smugglers used to run their boats in here: it's a perfect natural harbour. A boat might come in and anchor under the lee of the rock, and people sailing past would be none the wiser. So a sort of story grew up round it. As a matter of fact, there were never any smugglers at all."

Dicky Atherton told him he was an unsentimental beggar. "A pity to spoil a good yarn," he said. "Think how tourists would lap it up!" At which Harry shuddered, and uttered pious thanks that, so far, tourists had not discovered their part of the coast.

We went home slowly in the early evening, turning our backs upon a sunset that made sea and sky a glory of scarlet and gold. It had been a merry day, apart from the mishap that might so easily have ended in tragedy: but since Jack was alive and well, we were young enough to forget our brief time of terror, and we sang lustily, if not tunefully, as the launches glided over the still sea. Jack, perched on the extreme point of the bow, was loudest in the choruses. I could see, however, that his wounds were beginning to stiffen; when we landed I hurried him up to the house so that I might cleanse and dress them properly. He wriggled with disgust at my scientific bandages.

"Much better give 'em a dab of iodine and let the air cure 'em," he said: at which I shivered. I hadn't had the heart to apply iodine to so wide an acreage of skinned boy.

"Comfortable?" I asked, as I adjusted the last safety-pin and pulled his stocking gently over the whole.

"Oh yes. It's all right. But I do feel an awful idiot, trussed up like this!"

"But nobody can see, Jack."

"No—that's a comfort," he said. And then he astonished me, for he suddenly slipped an arm about my neck and gave me a rough hug. "Thanks, awfully," he said. "You're no end of a brick, Miss Earle!"—and was gone.

CHAPTER VIII
I HEAR STRANGE THINGS

DR. FIRTH appeared next day after breakfast and borrowed me, with the children, for the day. Mrs. McNab was immersed in writing, and seemed glad to let us go. She had shown real feeling over the news of Jack's escape, and had come to my room at night to thank me for my small share in it. I had remarked that I was afraid she would blame me for letting him out of my sight: to which she had replied mournfully that if one had a hundred eyes it would be impossible always to keep Judy and Jack in their line of vision. Then she had drifted away.

We went off in high spirits, my own raised to the seventh heaven because Dr. Firth allowed me to drive. I had not had the wheel of a car in my hands since the good days when I used to drive father on his rounds; one of the bitterest moments of our poverty had been when we saw our beloved Vauxhall driven away by the fat bookmaker who had bought her. He couldn't drive a bit, either: he scraped one mudguard at our very front gate. Dr. Firth's car was a Vauxhall also, and it was sheer joy to feel her purring under one's touch. We went for a fifty-mile run before we came back to his house for lunch.

The house was a fine old place, of deep-red brick, half smothered in Virginia creeper. Judy and Jack evidently knew their way about, and they promptly disappeared towards the stables, where two ponies were at their disposal. It was with difficulty that I retrieved them for lunch, which we ate at a table on the verandah, in a corner shut in by a wall of climbing roses. A delightful old housekeeper, motherly and gentle, fussed over us. The whole place breathed an atmosphere of home.

When we had finished, Dr. Firth showed us all the quaint and beautiful things that his brother had collected. They were almost bewildering in their variety. One great room was given up to stuffed animals, far finer specimens than the moth-eaten relics to be found in the City Museum. There were marvellous cases of butterflies, mounted so exquisitely that they almost seemed in flight: others of tropical birds, and a particularly unpleasant section given up to reptiles, over which Judy and Jack gibbered with delight. In one room were weapons, ancient and modern, civilized and savage: in another, barbaric ornaments, set with rough jewels. I recollect a beautiful cabinet filled with fans, of the most delicate workmanship. So large was the collection that my brain was bewildered long before I had seen everything. I sympathized with Judy and Jack when at last they struck.

"They're all awfully wonderful and all that," Judy said bluntly. "But if you won't think us rude, Dr. Firth, Jack and I would rather go back to the ponies!"

The Doctor laughed.

"I don't blame you," he said. "There is really too much for one day. I think Doris has had enough, too. Some other time you must come and see the rest: just now, I think we'll lock them up again. Be off with you!"—and the pair raced away.

Dr. Firth returned the jewelled Tibetan belt-clasp he had been showing us to its blue-lined case, and locked the cabinet carefully.

"Mrs. McNab is convinced that the Wootong burglar will pay me a visit," he said, laughing. "I don't think so: these things are hardly likely to attract the average sneak-thief, though, of course, many of them are almost priceless. They really should not be in a private house. I mean to lend most of them to the Museum, and then I shan't feel responsible."

"I should love you to be burgled," I said, laughing—"and the burglar to find himself inside that stuffed Zoo of yours. Just fancy the feelings of an enterprising thief who turned on his dark lantern and found himself confronted by a python! It would be enough to give him a change of heart, wouldn't it?"

"It would certainly be worth seeing," Dr. Firth agreed. "If he dropped his dark lantern in his confusion and couldn't find the way out, there would be a very fair chance of adding a lunatic to the collection by the morning! That room is uncommonly eerie in a dim light. I don't care for it myself. The animals always seem to me to come alive when the light begins to fade: sometimes you'd swear you saw one move. They say my brother used to sit there in the evening—he said the animals were companionable!"

"It was a queer taste," I said.

"An unhealthy one, I think. No—they're out of place in an ordinary man's home. And the servants hate them; not one of the maids would go near that room after dark if you offered her double wages. That big room could be put to much better use than housing those silent avenues of watching beasts. It would make a fine ballroom, wouldn't it, Doris?"

"Oh, wouldn't it!" I cried.

"I'd like to see it a ballroom," he said, putting his keys into his pocket, and leading the way out to the verandah. "I want to see young people round me, Doris: the place is altogether too lonely and silent. I'll clear all the beasts out before the next holidays, and you and Madge and Colin must come down here and we'll fill the house with cheery boys and girls. I think we could manage a pretty good time, don't you?"

"It sounds too good to be true!" I answered. "But I would love to think it might happen."

"We'll make it happen," Dr. Firth said. "You three are to be my property, in a way; you're the nearest approach to nieces and nephews that I have—and, indeed, I don't believe that any nieces and nephews of my own could have been as much to me as Denis's children." He put me into a comfortable chair. "Now you have got to tell me all about him," he said. "I never could hear too much of Denis."

I certainly could never have grown weary of talking. It seemed to bring Father very near to be telling everything about him to this man whom he had loved: who sat, leaning forward in his chair, letting his pipe go out as he listened. I told him how dear and good Father had been to us after Mother had died, when Madge was a very little girl: how, busy as he was, he had always made time to be with us, and had set himself to make our home what Mother would have liked it to be—a place of love and happiness. I told him of our camping-out holidays in the bush; of the half-hour before bed-time that he always kept free for us; of how he used to come to tuck us in, when we were in bed, and say "God bless you," just as Mother would have done. There were so many dear and merry memories of which it was happiness to tell. It was not so easy to speak of the last dreadful days, when we had all, in our bewilderment, been unable to realize that he was going away from us for ever.

"But he did not know, himself," I said. "It was all so quick: unconsciousness came so soon. We have always been thankful that he did not know."

"I wish I had been there," Dr. Firth said. "You three children, to face everything!"

He walked up and down for a few minutes saying nothing. Then he came back and put his hand on my shoulder.

"You seem to have faced things like men, at all events," he said. "And in future, you have got to count me in: I'm not going to lose you, now that I have found you. When you go back to Melbourne I mean to go too, to make friends with Colin and Madge. Colin and I used to be friends, years ago. He was a great little boy: the kind of boy a man would like to have for a son."

"He is certainly the kind of boy we like to have for a brother," I said, laughing. "Why, even his name helps to keep Judy and Jack McNab in order!"

"And that speaks volumes!" said Dr. Firth. "Not that you would call them extra-orderly now. Look at Judy, I ask you!"

The younger Miss McNab had just shot into view in the paddock beyond the garden. She was mounted on a nuggety black pony, which had apparently gone mad. Bucking was beyond the black pony, ordinarily an animal of sedate habits and calm middle-age; but it fled across the paddock, "pig-rooting," kicking-up, and now and then pausing to twist and wriggle in the most complex fashion. Behind the pair came Jack, who rolled in his saddle, helpless with laughter: his shouts of mirth echoed as he went.

"She'll be killed!" I gasped.

"Not she," said Dr. Firth. "That child is born to be hanged! But I would certainly like to know what had come to my old Blackie. I didn't think he had it in him to be so gay."

Blackie's gaiety at the moment seemed to border on desperation. He propped in his gallop, gave a series of ungainly bounds, and finally commenced to kick as though nothing else could ease his spirits. At each kick his hind-quarters shot higher and higher into the air, and Judy slid a little farther forward. At last, a kick so high that it seemed that nothing could save the pony from turning a somersault ended the matter for his rider: she left the saddle, appeared to sit on Blackie's head for a moment, and came to earth in a heap. The pony stood still, panting.

In their joyous career they had turned and were near the house, so that it did not take us long to reach them. I ran with wild imaginings of broken bones whirling in my brain: hugely relieved, as I came near, to see Judy gather herself up from the grass, rubbing various portions of her frame with extreme indignation. Beyond the fact that she was very dirty there seemed little damage done. And after all, to be dirty was nothing very unusual for the younger Miss McNab.

"That beast of a pony!" she uttered viciously. "What on earth happened to him, Dr. Firth? He just went mad!"

"He isn't given to excursions of that kind," Dr. Firth said, looking puzzled. "Blackie is always regarded as beyond the flights of youth. What did you do to him, Judy?"

"Only rode him. And I could hardly get a move out of him until just now. I told Jack the old slug wasn't fit to ride!"

"So he went and slung you off!" put in Jack happily, from his pony. "That'll teach you to be polite to a pony, Ju!"

"You be quiet!" flashed his sister. She cast a look of sudden inspiration at his innocent face. "I do believe———!" She broke off, and hurriedly unfastened Blackie's girth, lifting the saddle. A dry thistle-head, considerably flattened, came into view.

"You did it!" she screamed, and darted at him. Jack's movement of flight was a thought too late: she grabbed his leg as he swung his pony round, and in a moment he, too, lay on the grass, the injured Judy pounding him scientifically. We dragged the combatants apart, holding them at a safe distance.

"What do you mean by putting a thing like that under your sister's saddle, sir?" demanded Dr. Firth severely.

"Well, she wanted an exciting ride," Jack grinned. "She wouldn't do anything but abuse poor old Blackie 'cause he wouldn't go. She said he ought to be in a Home for Decayed Animals, and she wouldn't believe me when I told her he only wanted a little handling. So I thought I'd show her that he wasn't as old as he looked, and I put that thistle under the saddle while she was finding a new switch. And my goodness, didn't he go! Wasn't it just scrumptious when he kicked her off!" He dissolved in helpless laughter at the recollection, and Judy writhed in Dr. Firth's hands.

"It isn't fair!" she protested. "Just let me get at him for a moment!"

"Murder is forbidden on this property," answered her host sententiously. "He deserves hanging, but you had better forgive him, Judy, and come in for some tea."

Judy submitted with a bad grace.

"Oh, all right," she said. "Let's go—I won't kill him now, but I'll pay him out afterwards—you see if I don't, young Jack!" With a swift movement she possessed herself of Jack's pony, scrambling into the saddle and setting off at a gallop, a proceeding Jack vainly endeavoured to check by clinging to the tail of his steed, and narrowly escaping being kicked. He shrugged his shoulders, grinned cheerfully, girthed up Blackie's saddle, and went off in pursuit. They appeared together, presently, on the verandah, washed and brushed, and apparently the best of friends: and proceeded to demonstrate how many chocolate éclairs may be consumed at an early age without fatal results to the consumers.

We found a silent house when we reached The Towers at six o'clock, for the house-party had suddenly decided upon a moonlight picnic, and had vanished into the bush. Mrs. McNab did not appear at all: genius was working, and she had given orders that she was not to be disturbed. We dined in the schoolroom in unwonted quiet; the children confessed to being tired, and went off to bed early, leaving me free to answer long letters that had awaited me from Colin and Madge—long, cheery letters, written with the evident intention of making me believe that life in the Prahran flat was one long dream of joy. I was reading them, for the fourth time, when Julia dropped in to see me, on her way downstairs with Mrs. McNab's dinner-tray.

"I'd sooner be carryin' it down than up," she remarked, putting the tray upon the schoolroom table. "'Tis herself has the great appetite when she's worrkin': that tray was as heavy as lead when I tuk it up. Indeed, though, wouldn't the poor thing want nourishing an' she writin' her ould books night afther night! 'Tis no wonder she looks annyhow next day."

"No wonder, indeed," I assented.

"Well, now, many's the time I've said things agin her, but there's no doubt she's got a feelin' heart," said Julia. "I'll tell you, now, the quare thing I heard to-day, miss. 'Twas me afthernoon out, an' I walked into Wootong to do me little bit of shoppin', an' who should I meet but little Miss Parker—wan of thim two ould-maid sisters the thief's afther robbin' the other night. They're nice little ould things, them two sisters: I often stop an' have a chat wid them an' I goin' by. Little Miss Sarah she med me go in to-day an' have a cup of tay wid her an' her sister. An' what do you think them two told me?"

I said I didn't know.

"A baby cud have knocked me down wid a feather!" said Julia dramatically. "This morning, who should call on them but the misthress herself!"

"Mrs. McNab?" I asked.

Julia nodded.

"Herself, an' no wan else. Bence druv her in, but he never let on to annywan where she'd gone. She doesn't know them well, so they were surprised at her comin'. She didn't waste much time in chat, but told them she was terrible sorry to hear about the robbery. An' finally she brings out five-an'-twinty pounds, just what the thief stole from them, an' lays it on the table, sayin' she was better able to afford the loss than they were. They argued against her, but nothin' 'ud move her from the determination she had. 'Let you take it now,' she says, 'or I'll throw it in the fire,' says she. There was no fire there, by reason of the hot weather that was in it, but the bare idea made the ould maids shiver. So they gev in at the lasht, after they'd argued an' protested, but to no good: she wouldn't listen to annything they'd be sayin'. An' she lef the notes on the table an' wished them a Happy New Year, an' said good-bye. That was the lasht they saw of her, an' they was still fingerin' the notes to make sure they was real. What would you make of that now, miss?"—and Julia cocked her head on one side and looked at me like an inquisitive bird.

It was a queer story, and I said so. Mrs. McNab did not strike one ordinarily as a person of deep feeling or sympathy: and, despite the surroundings of wealth at The Towers, she kept a fairly sharp eye upon the household expenses and checked the bills with much keenness. It was difficult to imagine her going out of her way to pay so large a sum as twenty-five pounds to women of whom she knew personally very little. It just showed that one shouldn't judge anyone's character by outward appearances. Like Julia, I felt rather ashamed of having thought hardly of Mrs. McNab.

"Me ould Mother used to say you couldn't tell an apple by its skin," remarked Julia. "I'd have said plump enough that the misthress hadn't much feelin' for annywan but herself. She's that cold in her manner you'd imagine all the warrm blood in her body had turned to ink—but there you are! There's a mighty lot of warmth in five-an'-twinty pounds, so there is: particularly when you get it back afther havin' lost it. Mrs. Winter, she's as surprised as I was. 'To think of that, now!' says she—'an' only this morning the misthress was down on me sharp enough for all the butter we do be usin'. An' indeed, there's butter used in this house to that extent you'd think they greased the motor with it,' she says; 'but where's the use of scrapin', an' so I told her,' says she. Terrible stiff she was about it to Mrs. Winter. But you'd forgive her for keepin' one eye in the butter when she'd go off an' make up all that money to thim two poor ould maids."

Julia took up her tray and turned to go. But at the door, she hesitated.

"Tell me now, miss," she said. "Do you ever get thinkin' you hear quare noises in the night?—the sounds I was tellin' you about when you first came? I'd be aisier in me mind if I knew that some one else heard the things I do be hearin'."

"All rubbish, Julia," I said, laughing. "In a house with so many people as this place has in it, you're bound to hear movements at night some time. You're very foolish to worry about it."

Julia shook her head stubbornly.

" 'Tis no right things I do be hearin'. People like the wild young things that's in this house don't move about as if they were tryin' not to touch the floors with a foot. Bangin' up an' down stairs they are, makin' as much noise as they can—to hear Mr. Harry or that young Mr. Atherton you'd say it was a regiment of horse they were. That's the way people should move when they're young an' full of spirits. But the noises at night is very different—quare, muffled noises. If 'twas in Ireland you'd just say it was a ghost an' be done with it. Many's the good respectable house has its family ghost, just like the family pictures an' silver. Only there's no ghosts in Australia."

"Certainly not," I agreed. "You hear the trees rustling, Julia."

"Ah, trees!" sniffed Julia. "The other night I heard them ould muffled noises till I couldn't resht in me bed for them. I was that afraid, me heart was poundin' on me ribs, but I up an' puts on me coat, an' crep' out. Downstairs

I went, an' if annywan had spoke to me I'd have let a bawl fit to raise the roof!"

"And I'm certain you didn't find anything," I said.

"Well, I did not. But 'tis well known, miss, that them that goes lookin' for them sounds isn't the people that finds annything," said Julia darkly. "An' indeed, if I didn't see a ghost at all, I med certain 'twasn't only me that was afraid." She paused, looking at me with a scared face.

I was trying hard to be practical and commonsensible, but in spite of myself I gave a little shiver. There was something eerie in her tragic tones.

"What do you mean?" I asked, forcing a smile that felt stiff at the corners.

"I seen the misthress. She was huntin', too: she had a little flash-lamp, an' she came out of the smokin'-room, movin' like a ghost herself. Sure, an' I thought she was one for a moment. I'd have screeched, only me tongue was stickin' to the roof of me head! She looked up an' saw me, an' I cud see she was as frightened as I was. We stared at each other for a minute, me on the stairs an' she by the door. Never a worrd did she say, only she put her finger to her lips as if she was tellin' me to howld me noise—me, that couldn't have said a worrd if 'twas to save me life!"

"And what then?"

"Then she shut off her lamp an' went back into the room behind her. An' I up the stairs as if the Sivin Divils were behind me, an' lef' her to her huntin'. 'If there's ghosts in it, let you be findin' them yourself,' thinks I; 'sure, it's your own house!' An' pretty soon I heard her comin' upstairs slow an' careful, an' she went back into the Tower."

"I think you are worrying yourself about nothing, Julia," I said. "Mrs. McNab is often about the house at night—I thought I had caught a burglar myself the other night, and it turned out to be the mistress, coming up the kitchen stairs. I think she often wanders round when her work won't go easily: and she is nervous about the safety of the place, since the robbery at Miss Parker's. At any rate, if she is wakeful and watching there is no need for you or me to be anxious."

Julia looked unconvinced. I could see that she hugged the idea of a mystery. And, indeed, I did not feel half so commonsensible as I tried to seem.

"Why wouldn't she do it different, then?" she demanded. "If 'tis nervous she is, she might call Mr. Harry an' let him an' the other young gentlemen go huntin', with all the lights turned on, an' plenty of noise! A good noise 'ud be heartenin'—betther than that silent prowlin' round, like a lone cat."

"It might—but it wouldn't catch a burglar," I said. "Anyhow, Mrs. McNab might not have been after a burglar at all: she might have gone down for a book."

"She had not that appearance," said Julia. "Stealthy, she was: an' I tell you, miss, there was fear on her face!"

"I should think so—with you creaking down the stairs!" I said, laughing. "Probably she made sure that the burglar had caught her instead. And when she saw that it was you, she was afraid you might alarm the house. She's awfully anxious that the house-party should have a good time. I think it is rather nice to know that, even though she is working so hard, she watches over everything at night."

"I dunno," said Julia doubtfully. "Sure, I'd a sight rather she laid peaceful an' quiet in her bed, an' lef' all the lights burnin'. Burglar or ghost, either of them's aisy discouraged with a strong light: it's worth all the prowlin' a woman could do. Well, I've been lettin' me tongue run away with me, but you're the only wan I can talk to, miss. Mrs. Winter an' Bella, they sleep like the dead, an' never hear annything: an' if they thought there was either a ghost or a burglar in The Towers they'd be off like scalded cats, without givin' notice. An' where'd you an' I be then?"

"Cooking," said I with alarmed conviction. "For goodness' sake, don't say a word to frighten them, Julia! Do make up your mind there is nothing wrong, and go to sleep at night like a sensible girl. Lock your door, and if you hear anything, just remember that it is Mrs. McNab's house and she has a perfect right to prowl round it at any hour of the night."

" 'Tis great sense you have, an' you only a shlip of a gerrl yourself, miss," said Julia, looking at me respectfully—from which I gathered that I sounded more impressive than I felt. "Well, I will try so. But I'll be believin' all me days that it's a quare house, entirely!"

Somehow, I thought so myself, after I had gone to bed—the picnickers had come in, laughing and chattering, and then the house settled down to quiet. I lay awake, thinking of what the Irish girl had said: and, so thinking, it seemed to me that, gradually, queer, muffled sounds came to me: furtive, stealthy movements, and the creaking of a stair. Once I got up, and, opening my door very softly, peered out: but all was in darkness, and there was no sound as I listened, except the thumping of my own heart. I told myself, angrily, all the wise things I had said to Julia, as I crept back to bed. But I will confess that I switched on my light and looked under the bed before I got back into its friendly shelter.

CHAPTER IX
I BECOME A MEMBER OF THE BAND

"MISS EARLE—do you know where the children are?"

My employer's voice made me jump. I had slipped away from the drawing-room, where I had been playing accompaniments since dinner. It was a still hot night, following upon a day of breathless heat, and I was tired—in no mood for the dance for which Harry and his friends were now energetically preparing the room. Like Cinderella, whom I often felt that I resembled, I was hoping to make good my escape before my absence was discovered.

Mrs. McNab stood on the landing above me, looking annoyed.

"Are they not in bed?" I asked. "They said good night an hour ago."

"No; their beds are empty. And I cannot find them anywhere in the house. I—I have just come in from a—from a little stroll"—she stammered slightly, with a trace of confusion—"and I thought I heard voices in the shrubbery. I wonder can they have gone out on some prank."

"It's quite likely," I answered, feeling dismally certain that anything might be expected of my charges. "I'll go out and look for them, Mrs. McNab."

"You must not go alone," she said unexpectedly. "Change your frock as quickly as you can: I will come with you."

"Oh, please don't!" I protested. "I can easily find them alone, I'm certain. You mustn't disturb your work."

"I—I am not working well to-night." Her tone was awkward. "So it really does not matter—and I could not let you go alone. I would call my son, but that one does not like to disturb one's guests—and Beryl does so resent it if the children are troublesome. I have no doubt that we shall find them easily."

I had no doubt at all, as I hastily got out of my dinner-frock in my room. For, as I glanced from the open window, a swift flame flickered up into the sky, seemed to hang for a moment, and then curved and came back to earth, leaving a trail of sparks across the blackness. In a flash as vivid was revealed to me why Judy and Jack had been at such elaborate pains that afternoon to find an errand for me at the railway-station while they visited the one stationer's shop in Wootong; I had a mental vision of the queer-shaped packages they had stowed away in the governess-cart when we drove back from the township. Had not Colin and I burned our fingers over forbidden fireworks in the days of our wild youth?

"I think I have tracked them," I said, laughing, as I rejoined Mrs. McNab. "There are bangings and poppings coming from the shrubbery, and I saw a rocket above the trees. I think they must be holding a private Fifth of November celebration."

"Fireworks!" exclaimed Mrs. McNab, aghast. "But they are *never* permitted!"

I kept my face grave, but it was an effort. If Judy and Jack had restricted their energies to the list of permitted things, their lives would have been on very different—and much duller—lines. Compared with some of their highly-original occupations, a little indulgence in fireworks seemed mild. But Mrs. McNab was extraordinarily concerned.

"We must hurry," she said, darting out of a side-door with a swift energy that recalled the night on the shore when she had swooped upon Jack and spanked him with such unsuspected vigour. "I have an especial dread of fireworks in the hands of children. The figures, my dear Miss Earle, of accidents to American children who celebrate their Fourth of July with firework displays, are harrowing in the extreme. Death and disfigurement are common—terribly common."

"They do things on such a grand scale in America," I ventured, trotting beside her. "I don't think Judy would let Jack run any risk."

"One never knows," returned Judy's mother, gloomily. "Not with Judith. Even if she protected Jack, she would not hesitate to run any risk herself. And fireworks are so very unexpected. One cannot possibly——"

Bang!

Something exploded close to us, in the very heart of a dense pittosporum tree. For a moment sparks glittered among its myriad leaves: and then hundreds of sparrows, which made their nightly home in its heart, flew wildly out, chirping, twittering, terrified. We were the centre of a cloud of fluttering little bodies; they struck against our faces, so that we had to shelter our eyes with our hands. Above the clamour of the bird-panic rose smothered shrieks and gurgles of delight from Judy and Jack, unseen among the bushes.

"Crikey, that was a beauty, Ju!" came Jack's voice.

"Jack!" uttered his mother in awful accents.

"Judy! It's Mother! Grab 'em and run!"

A dim light guided us round the pittosporum, and Mrs. McNab darted towards it. I followed, choking with laughter. A smoky lantern, hanging on a bough, showed the culprits racing towards a heap of fireworks that lay on the ground within the murky circle of light. Near them Jack caught his foot in a creeper and pitched headlong on his face. Judy halted in her stride and darted to pick him up.

And then something happened.

Near the little heap of forbidden delight a cracker that had been lit and tossed aside as useless decided to fulfil its destiny and explode. It was a large cracker, and it did so with vehemence. A shower of sparks fell on a long trail of soft tissue-paper which had formed the wrapping of the parcel; dry as tinder, and sprinkled with loose gunpowder, it flared into flame, and a little breath of wind carried it fairly across the heap of fireworks. There was a quick spitting and hissing as the fuses caught. I seized Jack, who uttered a wail and sprang to save what he could.

"No, you don't, old chap!" I said, tightening my grip against his struggles.

A string of crackers went off in a spitting volley, and a Catherine-wheel suddenly began to revolve madly in the grass. Then everything caught at once. Rockets dug themselves into the ground, exploding harmlessly, while whizz-bangs and Roman candles and basket-bombs leaped and sputtered and banged in a whirl of rainbow sparks. It was a lavish and uplifting spectacle, produced for our benefit regardless of expense. But the producers wailed aloud in their despair.

"They cost every bit of pocket-money we had!" grieved Jack. "I could have got half of them away if you'd given me a chance! Why on earth do you want to come round poking your noses in?"

"We never get a show," said Judy mournfully. "We're just hunted down like mad dogs! I should think persons of twelve and thirteen can be trusted to do a few little things alone, occasionally, anyhow!"

She twisted round, and suddenly screamed. A long tongue of flame, a licking, fiery tongue, ran up her thin frock, and in an instant it was blazing fiercely. I dropped Jack and sprang to catch her, flinging her down; Mrs. McNab, quicker than I, was beating at the burning silk. It was over more quickly than one can tell of it. Judy, very white, sat on the ground in the blackened remnants of her frock, while we gasped and hunted for vagrant sparks. Jack burst into a terrified howl, rather pitiful to hear.

"Oh, shut up, Jack!" Judy said. "I'm not killed. But I 'specs I would have been but for Mother and Miss Earle."

"Are you hurt, Judy?" her mother asked, her voice shaking.

"Not a bit—I'm not even singed, I think. Jolly sight luckier than I deserve to be. I guess I can't talk much about taking care of myself, can I?"

"Judith," said Mrs. McNab, solemnly—her solemnity rather handicapped by the fact that she had passed a blackened hand across her face—"have I not warned you from your childhood that in the event of clothes catching fire one must cause the person in danger to assume an horizontal position?"

"You have, Mother," responded Judy. "And I stayed vertical—and ran. Well, I'm a fool, that's all!"

To this there seemed no answer. Mrs. McNab, regarding her daughter much as an owl may who has hatched out an imp, rose slowly to her feet. Suddenly Judy's defiant look changed to one of swift concern. She sprang towards her mother.

"I say, Mother—you're hurt!"

"My hand is a little burned, I think," said Mrs. McNab quietly. She held out her left palm, on which big blisters were already forming.

"Oh, I am a beast!" uttered Judy. "Mother, dear, I'm so sorry! It's all my silly fault. Is it very bad?"

"It is rather painful," Mrs. McNab admitted. She swayed a little, and I put my arm round her.

"Do sit down," I begged. "I'll run in for dressings."

"No, I am quite able to come with you," she said. "There is no need to alarm anyone. Just give me your arm, and I will walk slowly."

We gained the house unseen, a sorry little procession, and Mrs. McNab sent the disconsolate youngsters to bed while I dressed and bandaged her hand. The burns were painful enough, but not serious; my patient made light of them, and refused any stimulant except coffee, which she permitted me to prepare for her, after some argument. We drank it together, in the kitchen.

"Being bandaged is the worst infliction," she said. "I do not take kindly to being even partly helpless. I shall have to ask your assistance in dressing, I am afraid, Miss Earle. It is fortunate that I conformed to the fashion and had my hair cut—not that I might be in the fashion, needless to say, but because I was thankful to be relieved of the weight of my hair. It sadly hampered my work, and I have never regretted that I sacrificed it, even though I have heard Judith remark that I now resemble a turkey-hen."

This was one of the remarks to which there seemed no tactful reply. At any rate, I had none handy, so I merely murmured that I should be delighted to assist in her toilet.

"I will not ask you to come up to the Tower rooms," she said. "Perhaps you will allow me to come to your room when I need a little help. I should be glad, too, if nothing is said about the children's escapade. They have had a very severe fright, and I do not want them blamed by the household. There is an old proverb about 'a dog with a bad name'—and I cannot but feel that my poor Judith and Jack have suffered by their mother's absorption in her work for some years. My daughter Beryl's remarks about to-night's occurrence would certainly be very severe. I think we may spare them any further punishment, Miss Earle."

"I'm awfully glad," I said—forgetting, in my haste, that well-brought-up governesses do not say 'awfully.' Luckily Mrs. McNab appeared not to notice my lapse. "They are very sorry, I know. May I tell them, Mrs. McNab?"

"Do—or they will certainly blurt it out themselves. I will go to bed now, and I think you should do the same as soon as possible." She refused any further help, saying that she was quite able to manage alone. I watched her mount the stairs slowly, and then went off with my message for the culprits, whom I found sitting together on Jack's bed, steeped in woe. They received my news with relief, though it did not dispel their gloom.

"Jolly decent of Mother," Judy said: "Beryl and Harry would have been beasts—'specially Beryl. Not that we don't deserve it; but I can't stick Beryl's way of telling us we're worms. Even if you feel wormy you don't want it rubbed in. And every one else would have despised us." She looked at me keenly. "Did you ask Mother not to tell, Miss Earle?"

"Indeed, I didn't," I hastened to assure her. "But I was ever so glad that she said she wouldn't."

Judy's lip quivered, and suddenly she broke into hard, choked sobbing. It isn't a pleasant thing to see the complete surrender of a person who ordinarily shows no feeling whatever: I put my arm round her, not far removed from tears myself, and was not surprised when Jack buried his face in the pillow and howled too.

"Oh, you poor kids!" I uttered, entirely forgetting that I was a governess. They seemed to forget it too, for they clung to me desperately, and I hugged them and lent them my handkerchief in turn, since neither possessed one. When they began to pull themselves together, and to look shame-faced, I slipped away to the kitchen and came back with some cake and hot milk, over which they became comparatively cheerful.

"If you ask me," said Jack, "it was a pretty hard-luck night. If you and Mother hadn't smelt us out we'd have had our fireworks without any accident. Why, Ju and I have used fireworks since we were kids!"

"Rather!" agreed Judy. "And when they did go off in a general mix-up, there was no need for me to catch fire. Why did it want to happen, I'd like to know?"

"And when it happened it was bad luck that your Mother got burned," I supported. "Some bad-tempered gnome was certainly taking the place of your fairy godmother to-night, chickens. Only none of it would have happened at all if you hadn't gone out when you were supposed to be in bed. You didn't have much luck the last time, either, did you, Jack?"

They regarded me, wide-eyed.

"How—did—you—know?" uttered Jack.

"I was there—in a bush," I said, laughing. "But it didn't seem necessary for me to interfere, for you certainly got all that was coming to you, didn't you?"

"My Aunt, I did!" Jack said. "And you never said a thing! Why, all our other governesses would have sung hymns of joy!"

"From this out," said Judy solemnly, "I refuse to look on you as a governess. You are a Member of the Band. Isn't she, Jack?"

"Rather!" said Jack. "Will you, Miss Earle?"

"I will," I said. "But if I belong to the Band, the Band has got to play the game. No more night excursions unless I go too. Is it a bargain?"

They said it was, and we shook hands with all formality.

"We'll back you up no end," said Judy. " 'Means we've got to be horribly respectable, but it can't be helped, Jack." She heaved a sigh. "I've always known we'd have to be respectable some day, but I hoped it wouldn't be until we were quite old. But you've been an awful brick, Miss Earle, and we jolly well won't let you down."

"And when we're at school in Melbourne, don't you think the Band could meet some Saturday?" Jack asked. The outlaw in him had vanished for the moment; he looked just a wistful small boy, with the traces of tears still on his freckled face.

"It will be arranged," I told him. "And would you like my brother Colin to come to the meeting?"

They gaped at me.

"The 'record-breaker' Earle?" Jack uttered. "My aunt, wouldn't I!" He flushed suddenly. "Would he come, Miss Earle? You know you told us once he was jolly particular!"

"He is," I said calmly. "Awfully particular. But he will come, if I ask him. And I should like to ask him."

The original Members of the Band regarded each other with glowing eyes.

"Well!" said Jack at last, drawing a long breath. "We lost seven bob over those fireworks, Ju, but I reckon it was worth it, don't you?"

"Rather!" agreed Judy.

CHAPTER X
I HEAR OF ROBBERS

MRS. McNAB kept to the Tower rooms all next day. Julia brought me a message early in the morning.

"She put her head out at me when I did be sweepin' the landin' outside her door. 'Let you be tellin' Miss Earle I'd like to see her up here,' says she: 'an' I'll be takin' all me meals here to-day,' she says. 'The work is troublin' me,' she says. An' I'd say from the look she had on her that something was afflictin' her. Yerra, there's a powerful lot of misery over writin' books. I never did read a book if I could help it, but if ever I'm druv to it I'll be pityin' the poor soul that wrote it all the time. It's a poor trade for the spirits."

As soon as I was dressed I ran up the narrow stairway and tapped at the door. Mrs. McNab opened it immediately. She was very pale, and there were dark circles under her eyes.

"I have not slept much," she said, in answer to my inquiries. Evidently she had not climbed the steep steps to her bedroom, for there were tumbled rugs and cushions on the big couch; but she was fully dressed, and her iron-grey shingled hair was as neat as usual. "I think it would be as well if I did not go down-stairs to-day." But she laughed at my suggestion to call in the Wootong doctor.

"Oh no: my hand is really not bad. I suppose I must be feeling a certain amount of shock, that is all. I will spend a lazy day. You can manage without me, can you not?"

I begged her not to worry on that score, and proceeded to dress her hand. The burns were nothing to be anxious about: there was no sign of inflammation, and she possessed the clean, healthy skin that heals rapidly. She was mildly proud of it as I adjusted the bandages.

"I always heal quickly—no cut or burn ever troubles me for long," she remarked. "Indeed, I rarely have to bandage a trifling hurt: but one has to be careful with a blister. Perhaps you will not mind coming up after luncheon and dinner to renew the dressings. Judith is quite well this morning, I hope?"

"Quite—judging by the rate at which I saw her tearing over the paddock to bathe, half an hour ago," I said, laughing. "And she and Jack have promised me that there will be no more unlawful excursions at night. We have made a solemn alliance!"

"I am indeed relieved to hear it." She looked at me with something like warmth. "You manage them very well, my dear: they recognize something in you that they can trust. There has been mutual abhorrence between them and their other governesses. I had begun to despair of them—every one has regarded them as outlaws."

"There is nothing much wrong with Judy and Jack beyond high spirits," I defended. "And I think there is a good deal in what you said last night about 'a dog with a bad name'; they knew they were expected to be outlaws, and they simply lived up to what was expected of them. But they never do mean things, and I think that is all that really matters."

"I am glad you say that," Mrs. McNab said. "You are young enough to understand them—and yet I was very much afraid of your youth when you first came. But I have become thankful for it. You are a great comfort to me, my dear!" Which so amazed me, coming from the lips of my dour employer, that I got out of the room with all speed—to behold from my window my "misunderstood" outlaws vigorously watering Mr. Atherton with the garden hose—their victim having imprudently assailed them with chaff from a somewhat helpless position in an apricot tree. By the time he reached the ground he was so drenched that the only thing undamped in him was his ardour for vengeance. Judy and Jack, however, fled in time, and as the breakfast-gong boomed out at the moment, Mr. Atherton had to beat a retreat to change his clothes. Nothing could have been more lamb-like than my charges when I met them at the table. I decided that the occurrence was one which I might profitably be supposed not to have seen.

Nobody seemed to mind the non-appearance of the hostess, and the day passed uneventfully. Too much fire the night before appeared to have bred in Judy and Jack a burning desire for water; they spent most of the day in the sea, and I had the pleasure of seeing Mr. Atherton duck them both with a scientific thoroughness that seemed to repay him in part for what he had suffered before breakfast. In the evening they behaved with unwonted decorum—it drew anxious inquiries for their health from several of the party, notably from the girl who had found a frog in her bed. She announced her intention of making a very thorough search before retiring, remarking gloomily that when the children acted like infant cherubs a five-foot goanna under her sheet might well be expected. At which Judy and Jack smiled dreamily. They went to bed early, and when I tucked them up they were sleeping soundly, looking more innocent than any lambs.

Mrs. McNab came down after breakfast next morning, evidently rested. She made light of her bandaged hand, satisfying such inquiries as were made with a vague remark about the careless use of matches. It was a busy morning for me, for an all-day picnic was planned, and the preparations had to be rushed. Just as I came out with the last basket of provisions a motor came up the drive, and Dr. Firth got out. He greeted every one cheerfully, declining the invitations that were showered upon him to go to the picnic: he was too busy, he said, and certainly too old—which produced a storm of protest. Certainly he did not look old, as he gave back chaff for chaff. Not until the last car had driven away, loaded, did he look grave. Then the face he turned to Mrs. McNab and me was serious enough.

"I came with rather unpleasant news," he said. "There didn't seem any need to worry all those light-hearted young people with it, but I felt I must let you know. My place was pretty successfully burgled last night!"

Mrs. McNab went white to the lips.

"Dr. Firth!" she breathed. "Have you—did you lose much?"

"More than I care about. The thieves were discriminating: they didn't bother about anything bulky. They must have known a good deal about the place. All the unset jewels have gone, and most of the smaller and more valuable ornaments—some very valuable as rare specimens. I wish I had done six months ago what I intended to do next week—sent the lot to a museum. You were right in your warnings after all, Mrs. McNab." He smiled grimly.

"And you heard nothing?"

"Not a thing. I was writing until very late, and when I turned in I slept like a top. My housekeeper is a light sleeper, but she heard nothing. I am almost inclined to think that there was only one burglar. The police believe more than one had a hand in it. But I think that if a gang had been at work more would have been taken; to me, the small bulk of what has gone points to a man working single-handed. And I wouldn't be surprised if both thief and booty are in the neighbourhood yet."

If Mrs. McNab had been pale before, she was ghastly now.

"Why—why do you think so?"

"Because every one takes it for granted that he would get away. The Wootong police—not that they're especially intelligent—are quite certain on the point: they have been keeping the telegraph-wires busy with messages to Melbourne. I wish they'd show more anxiety to hunt the neighbourhood. How easy it would be for a man to hide his plunder somewhere in the bush and remain quietly here until the hue and cry died away! In the cities the detectives have a fair working knowledge of likely criminals. But a man could stay in the country, perhaps as a farm-labourer, without suspicion ever being drawn to him."

Judy and Jack had been listening open-mouthed. Now Judy burst forth.

"I say, I've a gorgeous idea! You and I'll be detectives, Jack, and we'll hunt round everywhere! We'll find out if there are any strangers about, and do some scouting. I'm jolly glad they wouldn't take us for their beastly old picnic, aren't you?"

"Rather!" said Jack. "Let's go and hunt through the tea-tree near Dr. Firth's!"

"Not if I know it!" said the doctor hastily. "You keep well out of the way, young people: there may be tracks, and I don't want them confused. I mean to get the black trackers down, Mrs. McNab: they may get on the trail, especially if my theory is correct."

"The black trackers!" ejaculated Mrs. McNab faintly. "Do you really think——?" She paused, looking at him anxiously.

"There's no harm in trying. Those black fellows are wonderfully quick at picking up a track. And I must say, I should like to put up a fight to get poor old Michael's things back. They're precious little good to me, but he valued them. Besides, if the thief or thieves should be in the neighbourhood, my house may not be the last to be robbed. He's visited the hotel and the poor little Parker ladies already: this may seem to him a good district to work in."

"I—wonder," said Mrs. McNab. "Oh, I should think he would have got away. He would not dare to stay."

"It might be less risky to stay than to go—knowing that every detective in the cities was on the watch for him. Of course, my theory may be all wrong, but I mean to take precautions. And I want you to be on your guard."

"My Aunt!" said Judy. "We may be burgled next, Jack. What a lark!"

"Don't be foolish, Judith!" said her mother sharply. "This is a matter far too serious for silly joking. Not that I really feel afraid, Dr. Firth. There is not much here that could be easily carried away, and I never keep much money in the house."

"No; but the thief might not know that. The enterprising gentleman who knew all about the Parkers' little hoard might well expect pickings in The Towers. I don't want to make you nervous, but it would be foolish not to be on the watch."

For all her attempt at unconcern, Mrs. McNab looked distinctly nervous, though she again expressed the belief that the burglars had got well away with their plunder, and threw cold water on the doctor's scheme of procuring the black trackers. I wondered at the haggard lines into which her face set as she watched him drive away—he refused her invitation to remain to lunch, remarking that all the Wootong police force were sure to be waiting on his doormat, eager for him to sign more documents. "I don't know how many I've signed already," he said, laughing. "It's a terrible thing to come into close quarters with the law!"

We lunched rather soberly: the children were repressed by their mother's grim face, and ate as quickly as possible, so that they might escape from the table. Mrs. McNab seemed lost in thought; she let her cutlet go away almost untasted, sitting with her fingers keeping a soft drumming on the tablecloth, and her brow knitted. I wondered whether the burglar-scare were troubling her, or if it were merely the perennial worry of her work: and wished I could escape as quickly as Judy and Jack, whose gay young voices could be heard in the shrubbery long before their mother rose from the table. She walked to the window and stood looking out for a moment. Then she turned to me.

"I hope you are not alarmed by this burglary," she said. "I really do not think we are likely to have trouble here."

"Then you shouldn't look as if you did," I thought; but prudently forbore to put my thought into words. Aloud, I said I didn't think I was likely to be nervous. Then I wondered was I right to keep silent about the movements I had heard.

"I think I ought to tell you that I have noticed unusual sounds several times at night," I began. I got no further, for my employer took a quick step forward, her face changing.

"What is that? *What* did you hear?"

"There have been rustlings and movements in the shrubbery below my window," I said. "Quite a number of times; and more than once I have heard steps on the gravel, sounding as though some one were trying to walk as noiselessly as possible."

She drew a long breath.

"Did you see anything?"

"Yes—just glimpses of a dark figure. But with so many in the house it seemed foolish to worry: anyone might have gone there for a stroll. I did feel as if some one were prowling for no good; but then, I know one is apt to fancy things, especially at night. Still, I thought I ought to tell you."

Mrs. McNab looked relieved.

"You are quite level-headed," she said approvingly. "And I am sure there was nothing to cause alarm: as a matter of fact, I very frequently stroll out at night myself, and I naturally try not to disturb anyone. A little turn in the night-air clears my head when I am at work. So, quite possibly I myself was your prowler."

"Yes, I thought of that," I answered. "Of course, there was the night I met you on the back stairs I was sure I had trapped a burglar that time!"

For a moment she stared at me with a look that seemed to lack comprehension. Then she smiled nervously.

"Oh yes—yes," she murmured. "Quite so. Well, I think we may agree that Dr. Firth's burglar has not paid us a visit yet. Personally, I do not think he will ever do so." She spoke hurriedly, almost incoherently. "And I hope you will not worry, or keep any watch at night. We have plenty of defenders, if anyone should break in. My son and his friends would welcome the chance of dealing with a burglar—yes, think it great fun!" The laugh with which she ended was a queer, forced cackle. Then she turned on her heel abruptly, and hurried out of the room.

I went in search of Judy and Jack, and, seeing them safely ensconced in the highest branches of a pine-tree, sat down on a garden-seat and gave myself up to thought. For the first time, doubts as to my employer's mental balance assailed my mind. Undoubtedly, she was queer; that I had known always, but never had she been quite so queer as in those few minutes after lunch. Was she really afraid of thieves? Perhaps, unknown to anyone, she had a secret hoard of money or jewels in the Tower rooms that she guarded so jealously: but in that case it did not seem likely that she would feel so sure that no thief would come. She would welcome Dr. Firth's black trackers, instead of trying to persuade him not to employ them.

And yet—I did not believe that any mere danger of loss would make Mrs. McNab look as she had looked; afraid, almost hunted. She was the mistress of The Towers, secure, guarded, wealthy: no outside risk could touch her. The more I thought, the more the conviction grew upon me that her mind was unbalanced. There had been something hardly sane in her nervous distress, her incoherence. And most of all I puzzled over her blank look when I had spoken of our midnight meeting on the night when she had brushed rudely by me. For, despite her quick effort to cover it, I was very sure that Mrs. McNab had not the slightest recollection of having met me on the kitchen stairs.

CHAPTER XI
I SEE DOUBLE

THE certainty that I possessed an employer with a mind more or less unhinged deepened throughout a long afternoon during which I found it difficult to adapt myself to the varying pursuits of my fellow-Members of the Band. To let Judy and Jack out of my sight would not have been prudent; they were filled with a wild yearning to go burglar-hunting, and, had they been alone, I think no warnings from Dr. Firth would have kept them from the neighbourhood of his house; wherefore I attached myself firmly to them, and tried to show that I was indeed qualified to belong to the illustrious ranks of their limited association. We played at burglars and bushrangers in the scrub—no game without some criminal element would have had the slightest attraction for Judy and Jack that day. I believe I climbed trees; I certainly crawled into hollow logs and miry hollows, to the utter wreck of a clean frock. Finally we decided to be pirates and possessed ourselves of the small motor-launch, in which we attacked and captured several of the small islands of Porpoise Bay, in spite of gallant resistance from the gannets and gulls that inhabited them. It was a bloodthirsty and exciting afternoon, and I should have enjoyed it had it not been for the turmoil of my mind.

I had the usual theoretical dread of anyone insane. But, somewhat to my own surprise, I did not feel at all afraid. Perhaps it was difficult to realize that any danger might be feared from Mrs. McNab, who, dour and grim though she undoubtedly was at times, was always gentle—if one excepted the night when she had so violently beaten Jack, down by the sea. That in itself, looked at in the new light, was like the sudden strength and fury of insanity. But it was only one instance. And, after all, many quite sane people must have wanted at times to spank Jack; Beryl would have said that the desire to do so was a proof of sanity. Apart from that one uncontrollable moment, Mrs. McNab had never been violent: she was only deeply unhappy. And, remembering her haggard face, I could only feel sorry for her. She was not an object of fear—only of pity.

The question of what I ought to do beat backwards and forwards in my brain while I bushranged and pillaged and led my band of cut-throats to the Spanish Main—as represented by Porpoise Bay. One could not go to Beryl and Harry McNab and express doubts as to their parent's sanity: it did not seem to be the kind of thing expected of governesses. If I wrote to Colin I knew very well that he would appear by the earliest train—even if he had to turn burglar himself to raise the money for the journey: caring not at all for the McNabs or their concerns, but only bent on snatching me from an environment so doubtful. Poor old Colin, who believed me enjoying "rest and change"! The thought brought a short laugh from me, which must have had something grim in it, since Jack, who was at the moment delivering an oration on skulls and cross-bones, evidently accepted it as a tribute to his blood-curdling words, and was inspired to yet higher flights. No, I could not worry Colin, unless it became quite necessary to do so: that was certain. Yet, it seemed to me that something must be done: if my fears were well-founded, I ought not to conceal the matter from every one. Then, with a great throb of relief, I thought of Dr. Firth.

Beyond doubt, he was the person to be told. A doctor, even if he did not practise, would be able to confirm my suspicions or to laugh at them as ridiculous: and he would know what to do. The heavy sense of responsibility lifted from me as I thought of his strong, kind face. I had a wild impulse to escape from the children and make my way to his house immediately; but common sense came to my aid, and I remembered that I had promised Mrs. McNab not to let Judy and Jack out of my sight. Besides, he might not be at home; and if he were, in all probability he would be overwhelmed with business resulting from the burglary, with policemen proffering him documents at short intervals. A little delay could do no harm, I thought, especially if I were very watchful of the children: the other inmates of The Towers could take care of themselves. He was sure to be over within a day or two: very likely to-morrow would bring him, and I could make an opportunity of speaking to him alone. So I tried to put away my anxiety, and to be a good and thorough pirate, as befitted a Member of the Band.

We became sated with bloodshed about six o'clock, and ran the launch home, singing "Fifteen men on the dead man's chest!" with intense feeling. Not one of the Band was fit to be seen, wherefore we sneaked in at the kitchen entrance and made our way up the back stairs, gaining, unobserved, the shelter of the bathroom we so sorely needed. Half an hour later we descended, using the main stairway, a well-scrubbed trio, clad in fresh raiment, so that we looked patronizingly on the picnic party, all of whom presented that part-worn appearance that follows a long day in the bush. They had just returned, and were excitedly discussing the burglary, news of which had just reached them. Several of the girls looked nervous, and declared their intention of sleeping with locked doors and windows— whereat Jack ejaculated "Frowsts!" disgustedly, elevating a nose that was already tilted heavenwards.

"Well, if they come here they'll get a warm reception," Dicky Atherton declared. "How about taking it in turns to sit up and watch?"

"Surely that is quite unnecessary, Dicky," Mrs. McNab said in a hurried voice. "The burglars are probably well out of the district by now; in any case, they would never commit a robbery the very night after they had broken into Dr. Firth's. You had all better go to bed as usual and forget about them."

I wondered did any of the others see what was so plain to me—her restless eyes, her hand that clenched and unclenched as she spoke. Surely they must notice her strained and haggard face. But apparently they thought it nothing unusual—Mrs. McNab never was quite like other people, and anyone might be excited over a crime so near at hand. Dicky Atherton laughed as he answered her.

"Well, that is true enough: I should think the beggars would lie quiet for a bit, anyhow, and we should all get pretty sick of sitting up for nothing."

"We'll go over to Dr. Firth's in the morning, shall we, Dick?" said Harry. "I've always wanted a chance of seeing black trackers at work."

"How do they manage?" asked some one. "You let them smell a finger-print, don't you? And then they put their noses to the ground and never stop until they've found the criminal!"

"Something like that," grinned Harry. "They're no end clever at picking up a trail from next to no evidence. It would be a lark if they tracked these fellows down to some hiding-place in the bush—I'd like to be in at the death!"

Mrs. McNab looked more troubled than ever.

"I think the whole idea of getting in black trackers is very foolish," she said. "It will only alarm the district and cause a great deal of unnecessary publicity. The daily papers always make a fuss about a case when they are employed."

"Yes, they think it's romantic!" said Dicky. "We'll have all the Press photographers down, and the place will be overrun with them, taking snapshots. We had all better go about in our best clothes, because if they meet us in a body they will attack us with their cameras, and it would be painful if 'Mrs. McNab's house-party at The Towers' appeared as we're looking now!"

"I will not have that!" Mrs. McNab exclaimed heatedly. "Harry, I insist that no one shall take photographs here—if you meet any newspaper people you are to discourage them, no matter what they say. To photograph a private house for a newspaper is an unwarrantable impertinence! Do not let there be any mistake about it."

"Be polite, if you must, Harry, but be plain!" laughed Dicky.

"I'll be plain, all right," rejoined Harry. "My boot shall, if necessary, defend the sanctity of our home! What are you getting in such a fuss about, Mother? I don't for a moment suppose that any newspaper would bother its head about us."

"Newspapers nowadays would do anything for sensation," answered his mother gloomily. "And I hate publicity given to one's private affairs: it is insupportable. They would drag all one's family history through the mire for the sake of selling a few copies." Her voice rose angrily. "This robbery is spoiling all our peace! I warned Dr. Firth, but he would not be careful—he might have saved himself if he had listened to me."

Every one was looking at her now curiously. Harry frowned.

"Oh, what's the use of bothering your head about it, Mother! It's not going to spoil my peace—not if I know it: or my dinner either. I'm as hungry as a hunter, and, thank goodness, there's the dressing-gong! Come along, everybody: I mean to have a jolly good dance to-night, burglar or no burglar!"

The dressing-gong was the signal also for the schoolroom dinner, so I herded the children upstairs, glad to escape from a scene that had had its unpleasant side. Looking out for a moment as I closed the schoolroom door I caught a glimpse of Mrs. McNab coming up the wide staircase. I was glad that she did not see me, for she was uttering incoherent words in a harsh whisper, with a little curious gesture of helplessness. There was a look in her eyes that struck fear into my heart. I longed for to-morrow and for Dr. Firth.

I kept my fellow-pirates with me in the schoolroom that evening. To go down to the drawing-room and be drawn into dancing would have been hateful to me; to my overwrought mind there seemed an air of mystery, almost of tragedy, overhanging the house, and I wanted the children to be where I could watch them all the time. They were sufficiently tired to be willing to remain quietly while I read to them. I remember the book was Newbolt's *Happy Warrior*, and when I had finished the story of Bayard we talked of the old ideals of knighthood and chivalry. It was the point I liked best about my outlaws that they were perfectly sound on matters of honour. A lie was to either an unthinkable thing, and they held very definite views about betraying a confidence.

"Father says that's the one thing a gentleman can't do," said Judy, who had no intention of letting the mere accident of sex exclude her from the knightly code. "He says that even when a secret is made public it isn't the square thing to let on that you knew about it beforehand."

My father had taught us the same thing. I felt my heart warm towards the absent Mr. McNab.

"Judy and I swore a Hearty Oath about it," said Jack, who was lying full length on the hearth-rug. "We said, cross-our-hearts we'd never do it. It's awful tempting, too, sometimes."

"Yes, isn't it?" Judy agreed. "I'd just love to be able to say, 'Oh yes, I knew all about that long ago!' with my nose in the air, very often. But it isn't done, in the Band. Father's a Member of the Band, too, you know. He won't let us swear many Hearty Oaths, 'cause he says they'd get cheap, and they ought to be solemn. But he approved of that one, and he swore it, too."

"He told us lots of secrets," Jack said. "'Cause he knew jolly well he could trust us not to split."

"Yes, he said it was good practice for us, even if we were pretty young. He'd say, 'This is confidential, kids,' and of course that was all there was about it." Judy's eyes were very bright. "Father's awfully splendid, you know, Miss Earle. He never asked us to promise to be good before he went away——"

"I spec's he knew that wasn't a bit of use!" Jack interposed.

"That was why. But he said, 'You're awful scamps, but I know I can trust you.' And we'd just rather die than let him down."

"Well, that is something to live up to," I said. "Bayard hadn't anything better. I think I like being a Member of the Band. Shall we have that meeting in Melbourne when your father comes back, so that Colin can meet him too?"

"You do have the splendidest ideas!" Jack said. They beamed on me; and when I went to tuck them in, later, they hugged me vigorously. My charges were not, as a rule, demonstrative people, and I was fairly dazzled by the honour.

I went back to the schoolroom, and sat down feeling rather at a loose end. Strains of the gramophone were wafted upwards from the drawing-room where the house-party were apparently fox-trotting with an ardour undiminished by either picnics or burglars. I wondered was Mrs. McNab working, or if she were prowling round in the night, a prey to her own disordered and troubled mind. Then I remembered, with a start, that I had not been up to renew the dressings on her injured hand. It was later than I usually went: probably she had been waiting for me, feeling neglected and annoyed. I was annoyed with myself as I ran swiftly up the narrow stairs.

The door of the lower room was partly open: a faint scent of Turkish tobacco drifted out. Since her injury, Mrs. McNab had left it ajar each evening until I had paid my visit: I would hear the lock click as I went back, before I had crossed the landing. Forgetting my customary tap, I hurried in.

The tall figure in the grey gown was standing by the window, looking out upon the moonlit garden far below. She did not turn as I entered and I began my apology nervously.

"I'm afraid I'm late," I said. "I'm so sorry, Mrs. McNab——"

The watching figure wheeled round swiftly. The words died on my lips as I looked: looked at the tall, spare form, the straight shoulders, the close-cropped iron-grey hair: looked most of all at the white, haggard face. It was the face of my employer as I had learned to know it during my four weeks in her house. But—*it was not Mrs. McNab!*

The moments dragged by as we stood, giving back stare for stare: I, bewildered, terrified, unable to move, the other grim and watchful. I caught my breath in a gasp at last, and a threat came to me like the lash of a whip.

"You will be wise if you make no noise!"

I could not have made a noise if my life had depended upon it. I could only gape and shiver, my eyes glued to the apparition that was, and yet was not, Mrs. McNab. Yet so like was it that I began to think it was my brain that had turned. Height, features, dress, voice—all were the same; and still, the face was the face of a stranger.

Then came quick feet on the stair, a stifled exclamation of dismay behind me, the door slammed—and I was looking at, not one Mrs. McNab, but two! Each the very counterpart of the other, they stood together, and I looked from one to the other with dazed eyes, utterly bewildered. Then my glance fell on the hands of the first, and in a moment light came to me. I pointed a shaking forefinger at those tell-tale hands.

"Why—you're a man!" I cried feebly.

The room began to swim round me, so that at one instant the two figures seemed to merge into one, and then divided and became two, four, ten, twenty, long, grey forms, still and silent. Faster and faster they whirled; and then came darkness, and when I opened my eyes I was lying on the big couch, with Mrs. McNab rubbing my hands. Beyond her, the other grey figure sat in her office-chair, smoking: all the time watching me with steady eyes.

"You poor child!" Mrs. McNab said gently.

That was almost too much for me, and I sobbed suddenly. The form in the chair became alert.

"Make her understand she must be quiet, Marie."

"She will be quiet," Mrs. McNab said, with a touch of impatience. "Don't be afraid, my dear Miss Earle: you have nothing to fear. You have only managed to blunder upon a secret, that is all. I know you will give me your word to keep it to yourself."

"Of course I will," I managed to stammer. "I am very sorry."

"So am I—for my stupidity in leaving the door open. I had run down to the bathroom for some hot water, and I forgot the door until I was on my way back. Then it was too late. I would not have had it happen for the world."

I struggled to a sitting position and faced them. There had been excuse for my collapse, for surely never were man and woman so amazingly alike! Save for the hands, and now, I could see, the feet, no eye could detect any outward difference. The man in the chair gave a short laugh, and rose.

"Well, I'll leave you, Marie," he said, in the low, deep voice that was the echo of her own. "You must get through a certain amount of explanation, I suppose—but don't let your tongue run away with you. This young lady has too recently graduated from the schoolroom to be oppressed with our affairs." He bent a keen, cold gaze on me. "I trust you are old enough to be able to hold your tongue."

"I have no wish to do anything else," I said, mustering what spirit I could; and, somehow, from that moment there was never the slightest confusion in my mind between Mrs. McNab and her duplicate. Like they might be in every feature; but in him there was a cold wickedness akin to that of a snake. I hated him then and afterwards, and he knew it.

"Well, good night," he said lightly, and vanished up the steps into the upper room. Mrs. McNab and I looked at each other, and there was something in her eyes that made me ache with pity.

"Oh, you are unhappy!" I cried. "I wish I could help you."

She caught my hand, holding it tightly.

"I am indeed unhappy," she said. "I will tell you about it—I know I can trust you."

It was a queer story—the kind of thing that I had thought happened only in romances. The man—Ronald Hull was his name—was her twin-brother: she touched lightly on his career, but I gathered that from his boyhood he had never been anything but an anxiety. Before the death of their parents he had been compelled to leave the bank in which he was a clerk, narrowly escaping prosecution for embezzling bank money. Then he had gone from bad to worse, living on his wits, constantly appealing to her for funds, always on the edge of trouble and disgrace. Her husband had established him in an auctioneer's firm in New South Wales some years before, and they hoped that they had done with him; but during the previous year he had again contrived to steal a large sum, and this time they could not protect him. He had been arrested, convicted, and sentenced to two years' imprisonment.

Her voice failed when she told me this. I patted her hand—never had I felt so helpless and so young.

"Don't you think you have talked enough?" said a cold voice at the opening above our heads. "I warned you to be careful, Marie."

"Be quiet!" she said angrily. "Do you want your voice to be heard?" She turned to me. "Go down to your room—I will come presently."

When she came, she was flushed, and there was a light of battle in her eyes.

"He is very angry with me," she said. "But you must know enough to make you understand. And I am worn out with silence and secrecy." I put her into a comfortable chair, and she went on with her story.

"We were almost thankful to know he was beyond the possibility of troubling us for two years," she said. "At least, so we thought; and my husband went away with an easy mind. But two months ago Ronald came here in the middle of the night, saying that I must hide him: he had escaped from jail, and was penniless and in dread of recapture. What could I do? I took him in—Harry and Beryl were away—and hid him in the Tower rooms. It was easy enough: I had for years been in the habit of shutting myself up here, and the place is like a little house in itself. I procured dresses for him, like my own, so that if by chance he were seen he would be mistaken for me—you have seen how remarkable is the resemblance between us. I pretended to be almost always at work, so that meals were sent up here—for him: and laid in a store of biscuits and tinned foods for the times when I had to be downstairs." She gave a weary little laugh. "One of the minor problems of my life has been the disposing of the empty tins!"

"And what have you lived on?" I demanded.

"Oh, anything. I had a good meal downstairs occasionally. Indeed, I have had no appetite. It has been ceaseless misery; the dread of being found out, the constant concealments and deceptions, the strain of being much with him—for he is no easy companion to live with at close quarters. Lately he has become very irritable, and almost from the first he rebelled against his imprisonment and insisted on going out at night. What I have endured on those nights, waiting here in fear and suspense! Of course, he was always dressed in my clothes; but I knew that sooner or later someone would meet him and speak to him—as you did one night upon the stairs!"

"Then it was he!" I exclaimed. "Oh, I'm so glad—I never could make out why you looked so cross and brushed past me so rudely!"

"I knew nothing about it until to-day," she said. "He forgot to tell me. And he encountered Julia, the housemaid, one night downstairs—he was thoroughly frightened that time, and made sure he was found out."

"And of course—it was he who caught Jack on the shore at night, and thrashed him!" I cried. "He need not have done it: the little chap was only playing."

"Did the children tell you?"

"I saw it," I said. "I had followed the children down, to see that they were safe. They have puzzled over your unexpected strength ever since."

"Ronald told me as a great joke," she said. "No wonder my poor little Jack was puzzled—I have not punished him in that fashion in his life."

"As a matter of fact, he said he respected you highly!" I told her, and she smiled a little.

"It might have made a difference in his feelings towards me if he were not a sweet-tempered boy," she said. "I was very angry with Ronald. Oh, my dear, if you knew what these weeks have been, you would pity me! The constant fear—the terrible uncertainty!" She shuddered. "There have been many times when I have been tempted to send him away and let him take his chance. But I could not do it. After all, though I cannot feel any affection for him now, he was my little brother once—just such a boy as Jack. That is the time I try to remember. And my mother left him to my care."

Her eyes were suddenly kind and soft. I wondered how I could ever have thought her cold—or mad.

"But how long is it to go on?" I asked. "You can't keep such a secret for ever."

"There is a chance of getting him out of Australia," she said. "He has a friend connected with a ship which will leave Adelaide next week—ten days from now, or thereabouts. It is a cargo-ship only, and this friend has promised to arrange a passport for him and get him on board, if I can get him to Adelaide. We have been trying to work out a plan to go to Southport farther down the coast; from there he could make his way up to the main line and reach Adelaide by train. But now we are afraid to move, for everything is complicated by the robberies in the neighbourhood. With the police on the alert—with those terrible black trackers about!—what can we dare to do? I am at my wits' end."

"But they will not come here," I said. "Dr. Firth's place is three miles away, and there is nothing to bring the police to The Towers."

"I do not know," she said slowly. She was silent, gripping my hand so tightly that it ached. Suddenly she dropped it, sprang up, and began to pace the room, wrapped in thought; and I sat watching her helplessly. The minutes went by while she went back and forth, like a caged animal. Then she came back.

"It has been a relief to tell you," she said. "I have longed to talk to some one—the thing has been too hard to bear all alone. Listen—I will tell you the worst fear of all."

"Each the very counterpart of the other, they stood
together, and I looked from one to the other with dazed eyes,
utterly bewildered."
The Tower Rooms]

CHAPTER XII
I HEAR STRANGE CONFIDENCES

BUT when she sat down she did not appear able to speak. Twice she opened her lips, but it seemed that no words would come.

"Don't tell me unless you want to, Mrs. McNab," I said, pitying the poor, strained face. "You are just tired out, and I know that your hand is hurting. Do rest quietly on my bed for a little while, and I will dress it."

To my surprise, she did not resist me. She let me put her on my bed, lying silently, with closed eyes, while I dressed her hand and bandaged it freshly. Then I had a new inspiration.

"Please don't move," I said. "I'll be back in a few minutes."

I ran down to the kitchen and made some strong coffee. Julia was there, sewing. She wanted to relieve me of the task altogether, and insisted on getting the tray ready.

"I'd not say 'no' to a cup, meself, miss, if you could spare it," she said. "This place do be gettin' on me nerves. There's the misthress goin' about all this day lookin' like a walkin' ghost—up an' down the stairs an' in an' out like a dog at a fair. Is it for her you're makin' the coffee now? But it'll get cold on you before she comes in."

I opened my mouth to say that Mrs. McNab was in my room; and then changed my mind suddenly.

"Why do you say that, Julia?"

"Sure I'm afther seein' her with me two eyes, goin' out ten minutes ago. Slippin' along by the back wall she was, in her grey gown, as if she didn't want to be seen. I was comin' in from the laundry, an' me heart rose in me throat at the sight of her—though the dear knows I've a right to be used to seein' her creepin' round the place. If she'd so much as pass the time of day to one, I'd not think her so queer; but 'tis like a silent grey ghost she is—never a worrd out of her. What with that, an' the thieves that may pay us a visit anny minute, it's no right place to be in: I'd take me pay an' go, if it wasn't for yourself an' Mrs. Winter."

"Oh, you mustn't do that, Julia," I said, trying to speak lightly. "When anyone is working as hard as Mrs. McNab she can't interrupt herself to talk. As for the thieves, I believe they are well out of the district; remember, the police are watching for them everywhere now."

"Yerra, the polis!" said Julia, with much scorn. "Is it the polis you'd be puttin' your dependence on, miss? Sure, as Bence says, they're too busy tryin' to catch poor motor-drivers to be doin' anny real worrk. Dr. Firth's seen the lasht of them jools of his, you mark my words. 'Tis meself was in Ireland when all the fightin' was goin', but I never felt as quare an' lonesome as I do in this place."

I poured her out a cup of coffee.

"Just drink that and you'll feel better, Julia," I said. "I'm not going to be scared of any thieves, and I don't believe you are, either. I'll take up a little saucepan: if Mrs. McNab isn't back I can warm up her coffee on my spirit-lamp when she does come in."

But I knew, as I carried the tray away, that it was not Mrs. McNab whom Julia had seen slinking by the wall. Ronald Hull must have come down the stairs very softly while we had talked in my room. I wondered what he was doing, out in the night.

Mrs. McNab had not moved, and for a moment I fancied that she was asleep. But she stirred as I came near her, and drank her coffee as though she were thirsty.

"That was very good," she said, lying back. "You are a very kind child to me: my own daughter does not think of such things. It is a shame to burden you with my troubles."

I told her not to worry about that. "Indeed," I said, "I have been more uneasy about you for some days than I am now. Ever since I have seen more of you, in looking after your burnt hand, I knew something was troubling you terribly, and I have been so anxious."

"Was it so plain?" she sighed heavily. "I have done my best to seem cheery and normal, but it has been hard; and all to-day I have felt almost as if I were going mad. I think and think, until my brain feels as though it were whirling in a circle."

She lit a cigarette and smoked for a few moments without speaking.

"Oh, I must tell you!" she exclaimed. "Now that I have once spoken I must go on and tell all. Your brain is young and clear, and you may be able to think of a way out."

"It won't do any harm to talk it over, at all events," I said, trying to speak comfortingly. But I felt appallingly young and helpless, and I wished with all my heart that Dr. Firth or Colin could be there.

"It is these robberies," she said. "I had no peace before they took place— but since then I have been in torment. I ask myself ceaselessly—*Who is the thief?* And only one answer comes to me."

Light flashed upon me.

"You don't think—you surely don't think—your brother . . . ?"

"I do not know what to think. Nothing like this has ever before occurred in our quiet neighbourhood. And stealing is nothing to him—we have had bitter proof of that. He needs money: I have raised all I can, to give him a fresh start when he gets away, but he grumbles at the amount and says it is not enough. Night after night he goes out, declaring that he must have fresh air and exercise, and I do not know where he goes. I have questioned him, but he only laughs at me. He knows his power over me—that I will not betray him—and he takes the fullest advantage of it."

With all my heart I yearned for Colin to deal with Mr. Ronald Hull.

Mrs. McNab leaned forward, crushing her cigarette between her fingers.

"And the danger is immediate," she said. "If any trail brings the police and the black trackers to The Towers or its neighbourhood, they may insist on searching the house. Even if Ronald denied it, I would not feel sure—he has lied so often. I do not know what to do."

"You would not tell your son?"

"Tell Harry? I could not bear to do it. He is only a boy, and we have managed to keep from him all knowledge of his uncle's disgrace: it would cast a shadow over his whole life. And I do not see how he could help me. No one can help. If I could get Ronald away to Adelaide at once—but he dares not go until the ship is ready to sail, for in any city he runs a grave risk of recapture. And there is nowhere else that I can hide him. It seems to me that I must get him out of The Towers immediately—but where can he go? Everything has worked against me—even this hand, with its wretched little injury that makes me half helpless. I had planned to take him up the coast myself in the small launch; with his aid I could have run it up to Southport, and hired some man to help me back. But there is no chance of that now."

"Couldn't I help?" I asked. "I know a good deal about running the launch."

She shook her head.

"You are very good. But I could not drag you into it. And, besides, it is not time to go. The next ten days are my great difficulty: I simply must send him away from The Towers. Picture his being found here!—with all this party in the house; the disgrace; the publicity for the boys and girls in my care. Beryl and Harry would never forgive me. It would ruin their lives; Harry could never go back to the University."

I saw that, and my sense of helplessness increased. To drag young Harry McNab into this tangle, just at the commencement of his manhood, was not to be thought of. I suggested Dr. Firth, but Mrs. McNab recoiled from the idea in horror.

"But he is the very man who has been robbed! He is kind, I know, but he is only human—how could I expect help from him! He would be the first to hand Ronald over to the police."

And then a bright idea came to me.

"Mrs. McNab—what about Shepherd's Island?"

"Shepherd's Island!" she repeated, dully. "I don't understand. You mean——?"

"To hide your brother. Very few people ever go there now, your son told me: no stock are taken there for grass this year, and the awkward landing keeps picnic parties away. The hut is quite weather-proof: he could be comfortable enough there."

"I would not care if he were not comfortable," said Mrs. McNab solemnly. Something in her tone revealed what she had endured at the hands of her refugee. "But—anyone might land there: he would not be secure."

"But he isn't secure anywhere. He might be found here at any moment, and then, as you say, all the household would be dragged into it. It would be no worse for him, if he should be caught, to be caught away from The Towers; and in that case no one need know his real name. And he could watch—he would have to watch; if he saw a boat coming he could easily hide among the rocks; they're full of holes and little caves. We could leave him a good supply of food, and take more over to him at night. And when the news of the ship comes it would be easy to take him off the island and run him down to Southport."

She stared at me as if I were an angel from heaven.

"You blessed child!" she uttered, "I believe he would indeed be safer there than anywhere. But how would I get him there? I am so useless now."

I was warming to my idea.

"You and I could take him. I can run the launch with a little help—just what you could give me with your good hand. Dear Mrs. McNab, it's quite simple! We could take all your tinned foods down to the launch—Mr. Hull could help, of course—with rugs and blankets. He ought to hide everything in the rocks during the day, in case of anyone's landing on the island. I should think he would welcome the chance of being there, after having been shut up in the Tower rooms for so long. And then you could laugh at policemen and black trackers, even if they came in swarms!"

She drew a long breath.

"It would be like heaven to think he was out of the house!" she said. "Oh, I have been desperate all day! But it is not right—not fair—to bring you into it. What would your brother say?"

I knew very well that Colin would say a good deal, but it did not seem worth while to dwell on that point.

"Colin would help if he were here," I said. "And as he isn't it's right for me to help. I don't run any risk—but if Mr. Hull is found in The Towers, think of what it means to your four children! And if he is on the island you will be in peace at night, knowing that he is not roaming about."

"Yes," she said—"yes! I would not wake each morning in dread of hearing of fresh robberies."

"Well, you might hear of them, all the same—which would be a sort of comfort to you, because you would know that your suspicions had been wrong. And it would not surprise me if they *were* all wrong—surely a man who is already in dread of the police would not deliberately do new things that would bring them on his track! It isn't common sense!"

"It would be a comfort to think that," she said. "I have tried to think it. But he is so foolhardy—so difficult to understand! My dear, the more I think of your plan, the more hopeful I feel. Surely on that lonely island he would be safer than he is here!"

"Why, of course he would. And every one in the house would be safer too. Do make up your mind to take him over, Mrs. McNab. Let us go to-night!"

"To-night!" she uttered. "But it is already very late. I—I have not had time to think—to plan."

"But there really isn't much to plan. There is moonlight enough to make everything easy: we have only to get the things down to the shore as soon as everyone is in bed. Mr. Hull could change into his own clothes in one of the bathing-boxes when we are ready to start. The launch is all in order; the children and I were running her this afternoon, and there is plenty of petrol. There could not be a better chance. For all we know the black trackers may be here in the morning."

She shuddered.

"Indeed they may. That possibility has been burning into my mind all day."

"Well, then, we won't have anyone here for them to find. Have you much food upstairs?"

"Quite enough for a week, with care, I think," she said. "He would not starve, at all events: and there is fresh water on the island. He could catch fish, too: if he made a fire among the rocks and cooked fish at night, no one would see the smoke. There would be no difficulty or risk about his being there unless anyone landed."

"And that risk is less than his being here. Remember, too, even if a picnic party saw him, they would probably think he was a lonely camper and would scarcely notice him. The police are not likely to think of going there—no boats will be missing and thieves could not reach the island without a boat."

"No," she agreed. "Well, no course that I can adopt is without danger; but I do believe that your plan holds less risk than any other. If he is captured I cannot help it—at least, I shall have done my best. I will go and tell him; I do not think that he will make any objection."

I had a moment's horror after she had gone, for I suddenly remembered that Mr. Hull had gone out—perhaps he was still away, roaming in the bush or on the shore: perhaps—who could say?—visiting some other house as Dr. Firth's had been visited the night before. Then all my excellent plans would be upset, and we should have to take our chance of what the morrow might bring. But I hardly had time to worry much over this possibility when Mrs. McNab came hurrying back.

"He will go," she said. "Keep a watch, Miss Earle, and come and tell us when every one has gone to bed."

CHAPTER XIII
I GO ADVENTURING

IT was lucky for us that all the house-party were tired that night. Dancing was often kept up at The Towers until long after midnight; but on this occasion the strenuous day in the bush had had its effect, so that a move was made towards bed soon after half-past ten. One strong soul cheerily suggested finishing up with a bathing excursion to the beach—and never knew what malevolent brain-waves I wafted towards him from my nook near the schoolroom door. Fortunately, Dicky Atherton poured cold water upon the idea.

"Don't be a lunatic, Billy," he remarked. "If you haven't had enough, I guess the rest of us have. Go and bathe by yourself, if you want to." At which "Billy" yawned mightily, and said that bathing alone was a poor game, and he guessed he'd go to bed, too. They all trooped upstairs, and I noticed that several locks clicked as the doors were shut. Evidently the girls had not forgotten the chance of the burglar. I wondered what would have been their sensations had they known that we were preparing to convey the suspected burglar out of the house!

I waited until ten minutes after the last light had gone out. The house was wrapped in deep silence as I stole up the stairs to the Tower rooms.

Mrs. McNab was waiting for me on the landing.

"Come in," she whispered. "We are all ready."

Ronald Hull sat smoking in her study. Something of the sneering coldness was gone from his face.

"You seem to be a most energetic planner," he greeted me. "It was a lucky chance that brought you in here this evening, though at the time I must admit that I thought it a precious unlucky one. Are you sure you can run the boat?"

"Quite sure," I told him coldly. I couldn't bear his face or his manner: he repelled me as a snake repels. It was difficult even to be civil to him.

There were many parcels and packages on the floor, ready for carrying. Mr. Hull was still dressed like Mrs. McNab, but he carried a pile of men's clothing over his arm.

"Well, we might as well make a start, if you think it's safe," he said. "This stuff will need more than one trip."

It needed three, since Mrs. McNab could carry very little. Laden like camels, we crept down the kitchen stairs, across the crunching gravel of the yard, and over the paddock, stowing our burdens in the launch that lay beside the little jetty. Backwards and forwards we went, almost running on the return journeys to the house: the dread of detection suddenly heavy upon us, so that every clump of tea-tree seemed to contain the lurking shadow of a watching man. Just as we were leaving the yard on our last trip, Mr. Hull well ahead with the heaviest burdens, a window at the rear of the house was suddenly flung up. Mrs. McNab and I stopped, petrified with fear. A voice shrilled out, that was unmistakably the product of the County Cork: a voice in which wrath struggled valiantly with nervousness:

"Who's there? Tell me now, or I'll loose the dogs on ye!"

"Answer her quickly!" I whispered.

"It is I, Julia," said Mrs. McNab in icy tones. They were really the only accents she could command, for she was shaking with dread; but they must have sounded sufficiently awe-inspiring to Julia, who ejaculated, "Howly Ann, 'tis the misthress!" and slammed down her window. We took to our heels and fled after Mr. Hull.

At the shore we lost no time, Julia's outcry might easily have aroused the house, and for all we knew we might be followed already; so we hurried Mr. Hull into the launch, not daring to risk delay while he changed his clothes, which could just as well be done at the Island. He grumbled a little, saying that he was sick and tired of living in women's garments; at which Mrs. McNab fixed him with a glance that, even in the moonlight, must have been daunting, for he broke off in the middle of a remark, and only muttered under his breath—Mrs. McNab took the tiller, and I switched on the engine. And it would not start!

The minutes went by while I tinkered with every gadget I could find in that abominable box of machinery. Mrs. McNab—how I loved her for it!—sat absolutely silent, betraying no sign of impatience; but presently her brother grew restive, and demanded angrily, "Won't she start?"—a query that seemed to me so singularly futile that I deigned no answer. I tried everything that I could think of, and still no response came from that very engine which had purred so happily on our piratical expedition a few hours before. Ronald Hull broke out rudely at last.

"I might have known as much! What fools we were, Marie, to believe in a self-satisfied school-girl! We might as well unpack the boat and go back—we can't sit here until daylight comes and somebody finds us!"

"Oh, hold your tongue, Ronald!" Mrs. McNab said wearily. "We are doing our best for you. And let me assure you that, whatever happens, you are not going back to my house."

He subsided at that, with an ill-tempered grunt. And then, I don't know in the least what I did—possibly my wrath communicated itself to the spanner I was using—but the engine suddenly began to spit, and then to purr. I heaved a sigh of relief, echoed by Mrs. McNab; and in a moment we were slipping away from the jetty and heading towards the opening of the bay. I took the tiller from Mrs. McNab, and in silence we shot across the moonlit water.

Having recovered from its fit of bad temper, the engine decided to behave beautifully. Its even throb was music in my ears. It was a still and perfect night, a night of moonbeams and starshine and peace, in which the load of anxiety and evil that we carried seemed to have no part. Beyond the headland, when we turned westward, the sea rose in long, gentle swells on which we rocked lazily as the launch sped onwards. Every tiny island was a dim place of mysterious beauty. No sound reached us, save, now and then, a seabird's cry. None of us spoke. Ronald Hull lit a cigarette and sprawled across the bow, looking ahead: beside me, his sister leaned back, and on her white face was the beginning of peace. So we travelled across the gleaming water, until Shepherd's Island loomed ahead, and I slowed down the engine, looking for the opening to the tiny bay where we must land. Soon it came into view. I ran the launch carefully beside the shelf of rock, and Ronald Hull sprang out with a rope.

We made fast, and landed. One after another Mr. Hull passed out the packages, until the launch was empty.

"You'd better go ahead with the lighter things," he said. "I'll change in the boat. Is it safe to show a light to guide me to this hut of yours?"

"I do not think it would be wise," Mrs. McNab answered. "But you cannot miss it—it is only a stone's-throw away. Whistle softly when you are ready, and we will come back."

We left him, and went up the slope with what we could carry. Mrs. McNab had brought a lantern, but, even had we dared to use it, we did not need it; although the moon was thinking of setting, the night was wonderfully clear and bright. We opened the sagging door of the hut to its fullest width and put in our bundles—I wondered if Mrs. McNab was as much afraid of spiders in the dark interior as I was, or if her mind rose superior to such earthly considerations. Personally, I cannot imagine any circumstances in which the thought of a spider in the dark will have lost its power to give me chills down the back.

A low whistle came to us as we descended the slope, and we reached the shore to find Mr. Hull arrayed in his own garments, and looking decidedly more cheerful.

"Thank goodness for my own kit!" he remarked. "Your clothes have been very useful, my dear Marie, but skirts are 'the burden of an honour unto which I was not born,' and I'm uncommonly glad to see the last of them. We'd better get this stuff up as soon as possible; you two must hurry away."

We loaded ourselves again, and returned to the hut. Our passenger was not excited by its aspect.

"Pretty dingy sort of hole!" he remarked, peering into the darkness within. "Thank goodness it's a warm night: I'll roll up in my blankets under a tree. There are probably several varieties of things that creep and crawl inside that shanty."

"You will remember to keep out of sight of the mainland in daylight, Ronald?"

"Oh yes—I'll be careful," he answered lightly.

"I hope you will. You should conceal everything in the morning, as soon as it is light—there are rocks and hollows all over the island—you will have no difficulty in stowing everything away. Do remember that there will be many watchful eyes along the coast during the next few days: you cannot be too cautious."

"Well, you've done all you can for the present, so you needn't worry," her brother replied. "If they get me now it will be plain John Smith they will get, who does not know of even the existence of such a place as The Towers, or such a family as that of McNab! When may I expect to see you again?"

"We will come in three or four nights—it is impossible for me to say exactly when I can get away unnoticed. By that time there may be news from Adelaide about your future movements. You will have to listen for the beat of the engine—we will try not to be later than ten o'clock."

"Right," he said. "Whistle three times when you stop, so that I may know for certain that it is your engine and not a police-boat's. I suppose you can whistle, Miss Earle?—you look as if you could!"

"I suppose you can carry up the remainder of these things?" I gave back icily. "It is quite time I got Mrs. McNab home—she is tired out."

"Let us go," Mrs. McNab said hastily. I believe she knew that I hungered to throw things at him. "Remember, by the way, Ronald, that if bad weather comes we may be prevented from taking out the launch—you had better husband your provisions. We will do the best that we can for you."

"You've certainly done that always, Marie," he admitted ungraciously. "I've no doubt you're deeply thankful to be rid of your Old Man of the Sea for a time. Well, I hope it will be for good in a few days—I promise I won't come back again if once I get to America."

I was already in the launch, starting the engine. Mrs. McNab took her place, and Mr. Hull cast off the rope.

"Good night," he said. Mrs. McNab answered him, but I pretended to be deeply occupied with the engine, and said nothing. We slid away gently from the rock, and in a moment the Island was only a dim blur behind us.

I believe we both enjoyed the voyage home, although scarcely a word was spoken. Mrs. McNab relaxed limply into her corner of the seat, smoking so slowly that twice she let her cigarette go out, when she would flick it away into the water and light a fresh one—she managed wonderfully with her one hand. As for me, I could have purred as contentedly as did the engine. It was good to be without that evil presence in the launch; better still to think that The Towers that night would be free from its blight. I liked to think how welcome would be the solitude of her eyrie in the tower to the tired woman beside me. Whatever the future might hold for Mrs. McNab and her brother, I firmly believed that we had done a good job in transferring him to Shepherd's Island, where his unpleasant temper would be restricted to gannets and gulls. It gave me serene pleasure to think how dull he would be. When Mrs. McNab recollected presently, with an exclamation of annoyance, that she had omitted to pack for him a good supply of tobacco, I fear I chuckled inwardly. I had small sympathy for Mr. Ronald Hull.

We swung round into Porpoise Bay and ran across to the jetty, slowing down to lessen the sound of the engine, and watching keenly ahead in case anyone should be prowling on the shore.

But there was no one: all was dark and silent, save for the waves lapping gently against the jetty piles. I made the launch fast, while Mrs. McNab gathered up her brother's discarded dress, and, hurrying across the paddock, we gained the house unseen, and felt our way up the dark kitchen stairs.

Mrs. McNab came into my room, closing the door as I switched on the light. She put her hand on my shoulder, and I saw that her eyes were full of tears.

"You are a very brave girl, my dear," she said. "I shall sleep to-night in the nearest approach to peace that I have known for a long while, and it is thanks to you. A month ago you were a stranger to me, and yet to-night you have done me a service I could not ask from my own son."

I mumbled something idiotic. Nothing that evening, unless it were the time when the engine would not start, had been so terrible as this!

"You do not want to be thanked, I know," she went on. "And, indeed, I have no words to thank you. But I hope that you will never think hardly of me for having allowed you to shoulder my burden—I know I should not have done it, but it was growing too heavy for me. You came to me like an angel of help. I hope you will always let me be your friend." She stooped and kissed me, and then, like Julia's "grey ghost," she was gone.

CHAPTER XIV
I FIND MYSELF A CONSPIRATOR

HARRY McNAB and two of his 'Varsity friends took a car and went off to Dr. Firth's immediately after breakfast next morning. They returned some hours later, much disgruntled.

"We thought you would be black-tracking all day," the girls greeted them. "Have you caught the burglars already?"

"There'll be mighty little catching done, if you ask me," was Harry's reply. "The black trackers can't come: they're busy on that murder case up in the Mallee, and can't be spared for a mere robbery. Dr. Firth's very disgusted. Of course the police are bobbing about everywhere, but I don't believe they'll do any good. There are two Melbourne men down as well—detectives."

"Very disappointing people," put in Dicky Atherton. "Not a bit like sleuthhounds in appearance. I expected to see something of the keen, strong, silent type, like Sherlock Holmes, but they're more like retired undertakers."

"And is there no clue to the burglars?" Mrs. McNab asked. I had seen the flash of utter relief in her eyes when she heard that the black trackers were not to come. She was looking better, but was evidently very tired.

"Not an earthly clue! The jewels and the burglars seem to have vanished into thin air."

"You can be jolly certain that they vanished into a high-powered car," remarked Mr. Atherton. "Burglars, as careful in their choice of valuables as these people were, don't do things in a haphazard way: I'll bet the whole thing was the work of an experienced gang, and that they were all snug in Melbourne, with their loot, before daylight yesterday. Well, it's a good thing that his loss doesn't trouble Dr. Firth as far as his pocket goes. But he's awfully annoyed at being bested—not that he admits that he's beaten yet, by a long way."

"No," said Harry. "I fancy that Dr. Firth will keep his teeth into the matter for quite a while. And it wouldn't be jam for the thief if he caught him. As Dicky says, it's the old chap's pride that seems most deeply hurt."

So we gathered from Dr. Firth himself when he came over, later in the day.

"The things were going to the Museum, in any case," he remarked. "So far as that goes, I am no worse off. But it is intensely annoying that, for the sake of a handful of jewels, poor old Michael's treasures are deprived of all their value as specimens. He was tremendously proud of them, and I feel as though I had failed in my trust as their custodian." He gave a little dry laugh. "I believe I feel it more because I really didn't care a hang for the things—a good horse or a good dog appeals to me far more than all Michael's hideous rarities."

"And what about the things that are left?" Mrs. McNab asked.

"I take no more chances. A man from the Museum is coming down to-morrow to oversee the packing of everything, and in a few days I hope the whole lot will be gone—I shall send them all down to Melbourne by motor-van, with the Museum man mounting guard over them."

"No need for that," put in Judy. "All you have to do is to put in a lion or so, and drape a few pythons round the van! Nobody will go near them then!"

"Wouldn't they look gorgeous, going through Melbourne like that!" Jack exclaimed.

"They would create a mild sensation in Collins Street," Dr. Firth agreed. "I'll suggest it to the Museum official. Meanwhile, I have two detectives about the house, both looking very wise and filling little black notebooks with remarks on the situation. Do you know, I have the queerest certainty that those jewels are not far off? The detectives scoff at the notion, but it remains, all the same."

"You have nothing to support the idea?" Mrs. McNab asked.

"Nothing whatever—it's just a feeling. I suppose Michael would say that his queer old jewels have a certain uncanny power of suggesting their whereabouts!"

"What's that mean?" queried Jack.

"Means they're magic, silly, so's they can tell you where they are," responded Judy.

"Hur!" said Jack. "Be a jolly sight better, then, if they said it straight out! Wouldn't the thieves get a shock if the jewels took to yelling 'Here I am!' whenever they tried to hide them!"

"It would be a great advantage to me," Dr. Firth said, laughing. "You two might keep your ears well open, in your joyous wanderings—they say that magic still lingers where there are children. An old fogy like myself would have no chance of hearing my lost property bleat."

"Is there a reward?" demanded the practical Jack.

"There is—I've offered £500, already, for the conviction of the thief. If you get the jewels without the robber the reward will be less, so you might as well make a thorough job of it."

"I could do with £500," said Jack solemnly. "I awfully want a yacht all of my own!"

"You're a nasty little grab-all," stated his sister. "People don't take rewards from friends, do they, Mother?"

"Certainly not."

"Oh well, the fun of getting them would be worth it," said Jack, though with some regret. "But you know jolly well you'd like that yacht yourself, Ju. Anyhow, I vote we start hunting now. May we, Mother?"

"I suppose so," she said—"if you don't go into very wild places. No, you are not to go, Miss Earle." She put a restraining hand on mine as I made a movement to rise. "They cannot get into much harm, and you know that you did not sleep well. Be home in good time, children."

"Right-oh!—we'll go and get the ponies, Jack!" They raced off together.

Dr. Firth looked keenly at us both.

"I must say that neither of you look as fresh as you might," he observed. "I suppose you have been worrying over this wretched robbery. You did not sit up on guard, did you?"

"Oh no!" Mrs. McNab replied hastily. "Harry suggested doing so, but it seemed foolish and he gave up the idea. I am really not at all alarmed about The Towers—we are such a large party, with several active young men: a thief would meet with a warm reception here."

"I think so, too. Still, if you should feel in the least nervous I would send one of my men over here at night."

This well-meant suggestion caused us both acute anxiety. The very last thing we desired was a guardian for The Towers at night. Mrs. McNab was so emphatic in declining the proposal that Dr. Firth looked at her curiously.

"Well—just as you please. But if you are not worried, I should like to see you looking rather more like yourself. Is the work going badly?"

Poor Mrs. McNab leaped at the suggestion.

"Very badly," she said, with a wintry smile. "There are so many interruptions—so much to think of throughout the day. I never can expect really free time during the holidays; although Miss Earle does everything in her power to spare me, and never spares herself." She patted my hand. "I do not know how much magic is in your jewels, Dr. Firth, but my good fairy was certainly at work when she sent me this kind girl."

Dr. Firth beamed on us.

"I'm delighted to hear you say so," he said. "One would not expect anything but kindness from Denis Earle's daughter. My luck was even better than yours, for you have her only for the holidays: I am not going to lose her again, if I can help it!"

"I should be very sorry to think our friendship would end with the holidays," said Mrs. McNab. "Indeed, after all the young people have gone away I should like to keep you here awhile, my dear, for a thorough rest—with nothing to do but lie about and read, or drive the car, or bathe. It would be dull, but I think it would be good for you."

"You're awfully kind, Mrs. McNab," I said. "But there's school—and Madame Carr. Think of the waiting twelve-year-olds to whom I teach deportment!"

"Hang the twelve-year-olds!" said Dr. Firth explosively.

I felt inclined to agree with him. For me, school and Madame Carr were only a fortnight away, and the prospect was a grim one. To see Colin and Madge again would be sheer delight, of course; but apart from those beloved ones I hated the very idea of leaving the country. My time at The Towers had been by no means all joy. Still, I had managed my job—that was some satisfaction; and I had made good friends, and had found Dr. Firth. And there were my dear little Judy and Jack. It was no small thing to be a Fellow-Member of the Band. I had yet to learn how big a thing it could be.

"I don't suppose the twelve-year-olds will be any more pleased to see me than I shall be to meet them again," I said, smiling at Dr. Firth's outburst. "Still, they are not bad youngsters, on the whole, and I feel so well now that I'll be able to tackle them in earnest. I was losing my grip before the holidays, and they were fully aware of it."

Dr. Firth said nothing, but he still looked explosive. It was Mrs. McNab who answered.

"I hope that if they ever tire you out again you will remember that you have a home at The Towers, my dear. And then I shall try to give you a time without any worries—only peace."

Poor soul—she looked as though she needed the peace herself. I was trying to reply fittingly when Bella appeared with the tea-tray and provided a welcome interruption. It was terribly embarrassing to have speeches made at one.

The next few days went by uneventfully. Judy and Jack scoured the country every day, returning in disgust at their lack of success in finding the jewels, but always ready to go out again. We saw nothing of Dr. Firth's detectives. It was hinted that they had a clue, a possession which Harry declared no self-respecting detective to be without; but whatever it was, it seemed to lead them nowhere, and the belief grew in the neighbourhood that the robbers had made good their escape, and were not likely to trouble the Wootong district again. The girls ceased to lock their doors at night; the Melbourne papers, which had given a good deal of space to the burglary, dropped the subject in favour of something more interesting. Only Dr. Firth still held to his idea that his jewels were not far off. But as nobody agreed with him, he said little, remarking that a man who had no foundation for his opinions was wiser if he kept them to himself. He was very busy over the packing of his remaining curios; load after load of stuffed animals left his house, to the unconcealed joy of his servants, who declared—Julia reported to me—that the place was becoming one in which a self-respecting girl could move about at night without her hair rising erect upon her head. "An' that's more than one can say of this place, miss," added Julia gloomily. "There's more than poor dead beasts is in it at The Towers!"

Mrs. McNab and I paid another visit to the Island on the fourth night, taking a fresh supply of food. We found our refugee in a distinctly bad temper, loneliness and lack of tobacco being his principal grievances. He became rather more cheerful when we supplied the latter need, but muttered angrily when he learned that no letter had yet been received from his friend in Adelaide. "A man can't stay on this beastly rock for ever!" I heard him say. "I'll be in a pretty fix if Transom slips me up, after all."

"You do not think he will, Ronald?" Mrs. McNab's voice was sharp with anxiety.

"Oh, I don't know. He seemed anxious enough to get me in with him, if I could raise a little money—but he could easily find somebody with more than I shall have. I'll believe in him when I hear from him—and the letter should have come before now. For goodness' sake come back as soon as you can, Marie; waiting in suspense in this hole is enough to send a man out of his mind!" He stood glowering at us as we left the Island. To my relief, he had not spoken to me at all.

I think that the doubt he put into Mrs. McNab's mind about the friend in Adelaide was the last straw that broke down her endurance. She had made very certain of the prospect of help from this man, Transom: Mr. Hull had never spoken of him, she told me, as if there were any chance that his offer would not hold good. I did not believe it now: I felt sure that Mr. Hull had only tried to worry her by expressing a doubt that he did not really feel. It was one of his pleasant little ways, that he liked to work on her feelings by dwelling on dangers, both real and imaginary: she had told me this herself, and I ventured to remind her of it now. But she shook her head.

"I do not know. He can be very cruel, but I hardly think he would be so bitter as that. It may have been that his talk of Transom and America was only a trick to induce me to raise the money—and I have raised all that I can. But if Transom fails, whatever can we do? He has been my only hope. Ronald cannot leave Australia without a passport—he dares not try to get one himself, even under a false name. And nowhere in Australia is he safe."

There was not much that I could say to comfort her. She gripped the rail of the launch, staring out to sea as we ran smoothly homeward: seeing, I knew, all that might lie before her: bringing her brother back by stealth to his old hiding-place in the Tower rooms, to enter again upon the dreary life of concealment and deception, with the ever-present risk of discovery, and of disgrace for them all. It was a bitter prospect. She looked ten years older when she said good night to me after we got back to the house. As I listened to her dragging footsteps, going wearily up the stairs, once more I longed very heartily for a strong man to deal with Mr. Ronald Hull.

It was not a surprise to me when Julia brought me word next morning that Mrs. McNab was ill.

"I dunno is it a fever she have on her," said the handmaiden. "She do be all trembly-like, an' as white as a hound's tooth. Sorra a bit has she seen of her bed lasht night; I'd say she was fearin' that if she tried to climb that small little ladder to her room it's fallin' back she'd have been. A rug on the sofy is all the comfort she's afther having."

"Well, she can't stay there," I said. "Miss Carrick left yesterday, Julia: we can bring Mrs. McNab down to her room."

" 'Twould be as good for her," agreed Julia. " 'Tis all ready, miss; as warrm as it is, I'll clap a hot bottle between the sheets, the way she wouldn't feel the chill. Let you go up to her now, for the poor soul's unaisy till she sees you. Herself sets terrible store by you these days."

There was no doubt that Mrs. McNab was ill—her appearance bore out all Julia's description. She tried to make as little of it as possible, declaring that she was used to such attacks, and that a day in bed was all she needed; she had taken the necessary medicine, and utterly refused to see a doctor. But she did not resist being taken down to the vacant room near mine, and leaned heavily upon me as I helped her down the stairs. I was thankful when I saw her safely in bed.

"Don't trouble about me," she said weakly. "My head aches badly: I am better alone. It will pass off after a time. But you must bring the letters to me as soon as the post-bag comes from Wootong—promise me, Miss Earle."

I promised, seeing that nothing else would keep her quiet. But when the mail arrived, the bundle of letters, which she turned over with shaking fingers, did not contain the one for which she longed.

"There is nothing from Transom," she declared tragically. "I am afraid Ronald's fear is only too well-founded." She turned her face to the wall with a smothered groan.

It was the longest day that I had spent in The Towers. There was scarcely anything that I could do for my patient—she had no wishes, and would take hardly any nourishment. Beryl paid her a casual visit, and then left her to my care—Mother was like this occasionally, she said, and wanted only to be let alone until she was better. Harry was more concerned, but accepted philosophically the view that he could do nothing in the sick-room and would be of more practical use if he kept the house quiet by taking every one out: and presently all the party went off for an excursion, and with the throb of the departing motors The Towers settled down to silence. Judy and Jack had gone treasure-hunting again, taking their lunch with them. There was nothing for me to do but sit in my room, going often to steal a quiet look at my patient, who generally lay with closed eyes, her face grey against the white linen of the pillow.

She roused a little towards evening, and permitted me to take her temperature, which I found far too high for my peace of mind, though the thermometer's reading did not trouble Mrs. McNab.

"Oh yes—it is often like that," she said. "Give me some more of the medicine: it will be better in the morning." She smiled feebly at my anxious face. "There is really no need for alarm, so far as I am concerned. The worst feature is that these attacks leave me so terribly weak: I am a wreck for days after one. And I have no time to be a wreck just now."

This was so true than any comment on my part was needless; I could only beg her not to worry, which I felt to be a singularly stupid remark. She took a little nourishment, and soon afterwards fell into a heavy sleep, from which she did not stir until after midnight. Then she woke and smiled at me, and asked the time.

"And you still up!" she said reproachfully. "You must go to bed at once, Miss Earle. I am better, and there is no need whatever for you to sit up any longer."

She was evidently better, and the temperature, though not yet normal, had gone down. I made her take a little chicken-broth and shook up her pillows, putting on cool, fresh covers.

"That is so nice!" she said, as her hot face touched their coolness. "Now I am going to sleep again, and you must do the same. I can ring if I want anything—but indeed I shall want nothing. Run off to bed at once, or I shall have to get up to make you go!"

I gave in, seeing that she was really worried about my being up, though I was not at all sleepy. Nevertheless, once I was in bed I slept like a log, and did not waken until I found Julia by my side with tea in the morning. She beamed cheerfully at me.

"Let you take your tay in peace, now," she said. "The misthress is betther: she's afther drinkin' a cup, an' she towld me to tell you to take your time, for she's needin' nothin'."

"Is she really better, Julia?" I asked anxiously.

"She is. There's great virtue in that quare little glass stick she's afther suckin'; she med me give it to her, an' she says it's made her norrmal. I dunno what is norrmal, but she says she's cured. The fever's gone out of her entirely. But she have a strong wakeness on her yet; sure I had to howld the cup when she drank, for there's no more power in her hand than a baby's. But that's nothin' at all: we'll have her as well as ever she was in a few days, if only she'll leave the owld writin' alone."

Mrs. McNab greeted me with a smile when I hurried in.

"Ah, I told Julia to make you rest awhile," she said. Her voice was still faint, but her eyes were clear, and the pain had gone out of them. "I am really better: the attack has passed off, and I have only to get rid of this weakness. But it takes time."

She was a very meek patient that morning. All her powers were concentrated on getting back her strength: she took nourishment whenever I brought it to her, and tried to keep herself as placid as possible by sheer strength of will. But strength of will, even as great as Mrs. McNab's, does not work miracles: she was still weak enough to tremble violently when I brought her her letters at twelve o'clock, and when she came to one in a dingy blue envelope her hand shook so that she had to let me open it for her. With a great effort she commanded herself to read it.

"It is from Transom!" she gasped. "Everything is arranged, and he wants Ronald to join him in Adelaide immediately—not to delay an hour longer than he can help!"

The letter fluttered to the ground and I sprang to her side. She had fainted.

CHAPTER XV
I SAIL WITH MY BAND

"I WILL not let you go alone."

"But I could manage quite well. It will be moonlight, and such a still night. There would be no real difficulty."

"I will not let you go."

"But it will be days before you are fit to move. You know you cannot risk the delay: it is your brother's only chance. You can't see it wasted."

"I can—if the price is too great to pay. I will not buy his safety at the risk of a young girl. I will not let you go."

"Then let me tell your son."

The white face on the pillow worked pitifully.

"No—anything but that! Harry is so young—and so proud. I cannot let him share the knowledge of disgrace. Life would never again be the same to him. I have tried so hard to keep it to myself—to spare Harry."

"Ah, let me go!" I said. "It would be so easy—the launch is ready, and the run to Southport would be nothing. Think of it—to have all your anxiety at an end! Say I may go, dear Mrs. McNab."

We had argued at intervals all the afternoon. At first, after recovering from the fainting-fit into which the arrival of Transom's letter, urging Ronald Hull to come without delay, had thrown her, Mrs. McNab had declared that she herself would be well enough to go out that night: a manifest absurdity, speedily proved when she tried to walk across the room. She could only totter a few yards, and then was glad to catch at my arm and let me support her to a chair. Again and again she had tried, with no better success. I put her back to bed at last, and gave her a stimulant, angry with myself for having assisted at the folly. And then had begun the argument.

It seemed to me that the only thing to be done was for me to take the launch and convey Ronald Hull to Southport. I didn't like the idea of doing it alone—who would? But there was no other way, since Mrs. McNab steadfastly refused to tell Harry. A second reading of Transom's letter showed us that we should have received it a day earlier, and that to reach Adelaide in time Mr. Hull must start that very night. It was now or never; and Mrs. McNab had made up her mind that it must be never.

She turned her weary eyes in my direction now with a hopeless movement.

"I cannot. It is absolutely unthinkable that I could allow it. Even Ronald's disgrace, sore as it is, would not be as bitter to me as my own conscience if I let you go. We must find some other plan of escape for him. I am too tired to talk any more. Promise me you will not try to go alone, and I will go to sleep."

I promised, reluctantly, knowing that she had already strained her endurance too far: she had a touch of fever again, and I feared that the next day would find her much worse. She looked relieved, murmuring something I could not catch; then she closed her eyes, and I went quietly out of the room, tasting all the bitterness of failure. I had so built on ridding her of her abominable brother. It was terrible to think that this wonderful chance was to be lost— that when she struggled back to health he would still be a millstone about her neck.

The sound of galloping hoofs came to me as I went out on the front verandah, and I saw Judy and Jack come racing up the drive on their ponies. They waved to me and shouted, but did not stop, tearing on to the stable-yard. I sat down on a garden-seat to await them—and suddenly hope flashed on me like a beacon-light.

Judy and Jack! They were only children, but they were strong and sensible, when they chose: they knew the launch and its engine better than I did, and the sea was their friend and playfellow. They would come, my little Fellow-Members of the Band, and ask no questions that would lead to unpleasant explanations. I could trust them, just as their father had said he could trust them—not to betray a confidence, never to let one down. It wasn't done, in the Band.

I turned my great idea over and over in my mind while we were at dinner in the schoolroom, and could find no flaw in it. I believed Mrs. McNab would find none, either. To go out on the sea at night was nothing to any McNab: that part of it I dismissed as not worth considering. The chief thing to ponder was the necessity of letting them into at least part of the secret: and there it was their very youth that gave me confidence. Harry, if told, would have demanded every detail: Judy and Jack would be content with what I chose to tell them, and I need tell them nothing that would affect their peace of mind in the future. I looked at my outlaws, unconsciously eating their dinner, with a gratitude that would certainly have amazed them, had they suspected it.

I went in to consult Mrs. McNab when we had finished. Before dinner she had not slept, and I had felt uneasy about her, for she was flushed and hot and restless: but now I found her in a heavy slumber, breathing deeply and regularly. She might remain so for hours, perhaps all night. Why should I tell her at all? Why not let her sleep on, untroubled, while the Band did her work? There was nothing to be gained by waking her. I knew where to find, in the

Tower room, the little suit-case that held necessaries she had packed for her brother's journey, and the money she had procured for him. It had been ready for days, in case of a hurried summons. I had only to take it, and go.

Slowly I went back to the schoolroom. The children were reading, their mother's illness making them unusually quiet; they glanced up at me, and grinned in a friendly fashion. I sat down on the table and looked at them.

"Do you remember," I asked, "what you told me your father used to say when he told you a secret?"

"Rather!" said Judy. "He always says, 'Kids, this is confidential.' Why?"

"Because I'm saying it now," I said. "I have something to tell you, and— 'Kids, it is confidential.' Is it all right?"

"O-oh, Miss Earle, you've got a secret! 'Course it's all right. Isn't it, Jack?"

"Cross-our-hearts," said Jack solemnly. "Shall we swear a Hearty Oath?"

"Your word is good enough for me," I answered. "But it has to be a very solemn word, because this is a big secret, and it isn't even mine."

"We'll never tell," Judy said. "Jack and I never tell anything, you know. Father understands that. Oh, Miss Earle, go on, or I'll bust!"

"You two have got to help me to-night," I said. "You have the biggest job that has ever come into your lives. And then you have to keep quiet about it for ever and ever."

"*And* ever!" said Judy. "Quick, Miss Earle!"

"I can't tell you all the details, because they are not mine to tell," I said. "But your mother has a friend who is hiding from some people who want to find him—why they want him is no business of ours. We will call this friend Mr. Smith. He is living on Shepherd's Island."

"On Shepherd's Island! In the old hut? Miss Earle, what a gorgeous thrill!"

"That isn't half the thrill there is," I said, laughing in spite of myself. "Mr. Smith wants to go to Southport—it is very important that he should go there to-night. Your mother and I were going to take him there, in the small launch."

"You and Mother! Nobody else knowing anything at all?"

"Not a soul."

"Do you mean you two were going out late to take him? All the way to Southport? Why, it's twenty miles!"

"Yes—to everything," I said. "But your mother has gone and got ill, and she can't come. That is worrying her dreadfully, because she knows Mr. Smith must be at Southport this very night. I wanted to go alone, but she would not let me. And all through dinner I have been wondering if my Fellow-Members of the Band would help me."

"Any mortal thing!" declared Judy. "What can we do?"

"You can run a launch as well as I can—or better."

"You mean——!" Light dawned on their eager faces. "You mean, you'd take us to Southport?"

"I mean that you two should come to help me take Mr. Smith to Southport. It has become a job for the Band."

"It's too wonderful to be true!" said Judy solemnly. "Oh, Miss Earle, you darling! When do we start?"

"I think we might slip out about nine o'clock——"

"Just when we ought to be going to bed!" said Jack, with a blissful chuckle.

"We had meant to go later, when every one was in bed—but I am very anxious to get back before your mother wakes. She is fast asleep now. If your brother or sister should come up after nine and find everything in darkness they will think we are all in bed. It seems to me the safest plan."

"I suppose I'm really awake!" Judy remarked. "It would be too awful to wake up and find I had only dreamed it! Pinch me, kid, will you—Ouch!"—as Jack promptly complied. "Yes, I'm awake, all right. Miss Earle, d'you mean that no one but you and Mother knows Mr. Smith is on Shepherd's Island?"

"No one."

"How did he get there?"

"We took him one night some time ago."

"What does he live on?"

"We gave him food. And he catches fish."

"Where was he before?"

"Oh—different places." The cross-examination was growing too searching. "Judy, I don't want you to ask me questions, dear."

"I'm sorry, Miss Earle," was the quick response.

"It isn't my secret, but your mother's. I am telling you without her leave, and she may be worried when she knows. I want you to promise to ask no questions—to try not to be curious, even though it's hard, about what really doesn't concern you two or me. We are only acting as agents, and it isn't our business. And don't ask your mother anything when she is better. It is a matter to be silent about—on the honour of the Band."

"Cross-our-hearts!" they said in chorus—a touch of awe on their young faces.

"That's all right, then. Just look upon it that you're doing a good turn and helping a lame dog over a stile—and, of course, one doesn't talk of that sort of thing afterwards."

"Rather not!" Jack said. "We're never to speak of it again, 'cept when we three are together."

"And very little then," I said. "I'm going to forget all about it from the minute I come home to-night."

"I don't s'pose we could do that, because it's the biggest adventure we've ever had in the world, and we're awfully obliged to you for giving it to us— aren't we, Ju? But it's a deadly secret for ever and ever. Will Mr. Smith know who we are?"

"He may. But he is rather down on his luck, and I don't think he will want to talk."

"Well, goodness knows we don't want to worry the poor beggar!" remarked Jack, in masculine sympathy. "Can I be engine-man, Miss Earle?"

"Yes, please. And will you steer, Judy?"

"Don't you want to? Oh, I'd love to—and then it'll be all our expedition and you'll just be the Admiral and not do any work!" Judy hugged me in her ecstasy. "We know Southport quite well, you see—we've often been there in the launch, so we can do it all ourselves." Joy overcame her: she jumped up and pranced round the room wildly.

"Judy, you villain, be quiet, or I won't let you be even a cabin-boy," I said, laughing. "You have got to be absolutely steady and silent—both of you. Now go on with your reading while I get ready."

I peeped at Mrs. McNab, who was still sleeping heavily; and then ran up to her study, the key of which was in my care. The suit-case was on the table: I glanced inside it, to make sure that the money was there. Yes, it was all safe— a neat package of crisp bank-notes, tucked into a stout envelope among the clothes. Locking the study, I carried the suit-case down to my room, and found a long coat, into the pocket of which I slipped an electric torch, with a dark veil to tie over my hair. Then I scribbled on a half-sheet of notepaper: "Gone with Judy and Jack—please don't worry," and put it on a little tray with nourishment: a glass of milk and one of barley-water, with a saucer of chicken jelly. Mrs. McNab did not stir as I put the tray on the table beside her bed.

"Please go on sleeping," I whispered. "I'll take great care of your babies." There was no sound but her heavy breathing, and I tiptoed out. I found Judy and Jack returning ecstatically from arranging dummy figures in their beds. We extinguished all the lights in our part of the house, and in a few moments we were hurrying across the paddock. It was barely nine o'clock.

There was no doubt that the presence of my two outlaws gave our expedition the air of a joyous adventure. Mrs. McNab and I had come in fear and trembling, seeing danger in every shadow; but with Judy and Jack I raced merrily down to the shore, and we stowed ourselves in the launch and pushed off with much ridiculous pomp and ceremony, as befitted a lordly Admiral with a crew sworn to be faithful. To the children it was simply a colossal lark, spiced with a glorious touch of mystery; it was easy enough to take their view of it and share their delight, until Shepherd's Island suddenly showed before us. Then we ran in silently, and I got out and went up the slope for a little way, giving the signal of three low whistles—at which I could feel the new thrill that ran through Judy and Jack. Three whistles—and a hunted man in the dark! And to think that we, who shared this wonder, had a week ago played at pirates, like children, with gulls for foes!

Ronald Hull came running down with long strides.

"Is that you, Marie?" he breathed. "Have you heard from Transom?"

"Mrs. McNab is ill," I told him curtly. "She has sent me in her place. The letter came this morning, and we are ready to take you to Southport, now."

"We! Whom have you told?"

"Nobody. I have Judy and Jack with me, to help with the boat, but they do not know who you are. It was the only way: you have to be in Adelaide as quickly as possible."

"But have you the money? I can't go without it."

"I have everything, and here is Transom's letter: you are to get out at Mount Lofty, outside Adelaide, where he will meet you with a car. Is there anything you want to ask me?—because I do not want you to talk before the children. Your voice is so like their mother's that it might make them suspicious. And please keep your hat pulled down well over your face."

"You're free enough with your orders," he said with a sneer. "However, I suppose I am in your hands. Where is the money?"

"In the launch, in your suit-case. Do you want to get anything from the hut?"

"Yes—my hat and a few things. Get into the boat; I'll be back in a few minutes." He ran back, and I went down to the shore, where Judy and Jack waited in a solemn silence. But the launch seemed to quiver with their ecstasy!

We carried no light as yet—the moon gave us sufficient to steer by, though clouds hid it now and then. I was glad that a bank had drifted across its broad face just as Ronald Hull came down, in a long mackintosh, with a soft hat pulled over his eyes. He took his place on the bow, and we edged away for the last time from Shepherd's Island.

Never was there a more silent voyage. Not a word fell between us as we ran the long miles along the coast, passing, one after another, the lights of little villages. The sky grew more and more overcast, and the air warmer, with little puffs of hot wind now and then. Had I been less centred on getting to Southport and seeing the last of my passenger, I might have been anxious about the weather; but I could only think of the blessed certainty that soon he would be gone, and hug myself with joy when I remembered the news I should have in the morning for Mrs. McNab. Judy's hand was light on the tiller: Jack crouched over the engine, a queer, gnome-like figure, in the shadow. Ahead, the sinister figure sat on the bow, his back to us, smoking. I wondered what his feelings were, with freedom opening before him: and hardened my heart anew as I recollected that he had made no inquiry whatever about Mrs. McNab's illness. Truly, it was a meritorious act, to rid a family of Mr. Ronald Hull.

"There's Southport!" Judy said softly.

The lights of a town showed ahead, scattered and dim, with a few standing apart that marked the pier. We ran in gently, slowing the engine. No one was to be seen as we crept alongside the pier, looking for the steps at its side. The launch scraped them presently, and Mr. Hull steadied her and sprang ashore, while I handed up his possessions.

"Thanks," he said, in a low voice. "Good night."

"Good night—and good luck!" I had to say that, because I was representing Mrs. McNab. But I fear that, so long as he got clear of Australia, I did not care in the least whatever might happen to Mrs. McNab's brother. I only hoped fervently that we might never see him again. It is years ago now, but he still gives me unpleasant dreams.

We headed for home joyfully, dodging anchored fishing-boats until we were out in the open and could go full speed ahead. Nothing mattered to us now: we had dropped our dangerous cargo, and not one of us cared who heard our engine as Jack opened the throttle and the launch shot over the oily sea. Judy was the first to speak.

"I did want to see his face, so's I could make him into a real hero," she said regretfully. "You can't make a hero very well out of a mackintosh and a felt hat!"

"I don't see why you can't," I told her, laughing. "It makes it all the more beautifully mysterious, like the Man in the Iron Mask. But you are to wash him out of your memory as soon as you can, and only remember that the Band had a gorgeous and exciting midnight voyage. As a matter of fact, this isn't a motor-launch at all: it's the *Golden Hind*, and I'm Drake, and you are my faithful captains!"

"And there's a Spaniard ahead!" quoth Jack ferociously. "Up, Guards, and at 'em!"

A hot puff of wind went by; and a dash of spray fell on board. I glanced round, to see a dark line of clouds across the sky.

"There may or may not be Spaniards ahead, but there's rain and wind behind," I said. "Get all you can out of her, Jack—I don't want to take you two home like drowned rats."

"P'f!" Judy ejaculated. "What's rain to us jolly mariners!"

We were to have an opportunity of seeing that. The clouds spread rapidly, and the wind rose. We were yet five miles from home when the moon was blotted out, and almost simultaneously the rain came down, in gusty squalls that deepened to a steady downpour. I took the tiller from Judy, who sat peering forward, picking up one shore-light after another as we raced the leaping seas. They were staunch comrades, my Fellow-Members: they sat as unconcernedly as if they were at dinner, efficient and cheerful, while I wondered what I should have done had I come alone, as I had wished. At intervals they apologized to me for the unpleasant nature of their weather, and hoped I was not getting very wet.

"We'll have to turn and run back against it pretty soon, if it doesn't clear," Judy remarked. "It won't do to get among the islands in this darkness."

"It's going to clear," Jack said, scanning the horizon wisely.

"Well, you just slow down," returned his sister. "I'd hate to hit an island at this pace!"

Jack grunted, and slowed down—and grunted again as a wave hit us squarely, deluging us with a rush of black water, just as the cover slammed down on the engine. That was the last effort of the squall: it lifted and blew away over the sea, and the moon came out and sailed majestically through the flying clouds, revealing the fact that we were quite unpleasantly near the islands which Judy would have hated to hit. Nothing troubled us now; we sang a song of triumph in whispers as we danced over the big seas and rounded the headland of Porpoise Bay. There is great solace in a whispered chant of triumph if circumstances prevent a full-throated chorus.

Drenched, but entirely cheerful, my outlaws and I made a burglarious entry into the darkened house. I had taken the precaution of leaving a big Thermos of hot milk, with which I regaled them when I had them snugly tucked into bed, after a brisk rub-down.

"That was heavenly!" said Judy, snuggling into her pillow. "I've had the most beautiful night of my life, Miss Earle, and I'll bless you for it always!"

"Me, too," echoed Jack sleepily.

"I rather enjoyed it myself," I said. "Go to sleep, Fellow-Members. I shall certainly tell Colin that if he ever wants two mates in a tight place I can supply him from the Band!"

"The letter fluttered to the ground and I sprang
to her side. She had fainted."
The Tower Rooms]

CHAPTER XVI
I FIND A LUCKY SIXPENCE

AS soon as I was in dry things I slipped into Mrs. McNab's room, my heart thumping. All through our voyage I had pictured her waking up and needing me: perhaps alarming the household, perhaps thrown into anxiety by reading my note. There were a dozen unpleasant possibilities, and I had explored them all.

But luck had held for me throughout that evening. She lay just as I had left her hours before, breathing deeply and regularly: the tray was untouched beside her, the note in its original fold. I pocketed it thankfully and went to bed—to wake with a start in the early dawn.

I threw on a dressing-gown and went across to Mrs. McNab's room. She was lying awake and greeted me with a smile.

"You should not be up so early," she said. "No, I am quite comfortable and better, and I have taken some jelly. And I feel cheerful, though I do not know why. I went to sleep so miserable, but a comforting dream came to me: a dream in which I saw Ronald, safe and happy and good. Is it not curious that I should have such a happy dream, just when all our plans for him are ruined!"

"I don't know," I said, and smiled at her "I think it was a sensible dream, sent as a warning."

"I would like to think so," she said wistfully. "But everything is so dark and uncertain now, and I do not know how to plan."

I suppose I grinned idiotically, for suddenly her face changed. She looked at me keenly, rising on her elbow.

"Miss Earle, you have something to tell me! You—you did not break your promise to me!"

"I did not," I said. "To go alone was what I promised not to do, and I didn't go alone. I took Judy and Jack with me, bless their dear hearts: they think we were assisting a gentleman named—possibly—Smith, and they asked no questions, and will ask none in the future. Thanks to the darkness they never saw his face. And we landed your brother at Southport before midnight, dear Mrs. McNab, and his money and everything. There wasn't a hitch, and he's well on his way to the Adelaide line, I hope."

For a full minute she lay and looked at me without speaking. Then she suddenly put her face into the pillow and broke into a passion of sobs.

"Oh!" I uttered, horribly alarmed. "Oh, please don't. Mrs. McNab, dear! I shouldn't have told you in such a hurry, but you guessed so quickly that something had happened." Dismally I felt that I had been a failure, and I nearly howled, myself. "I—I thought you'd be glad!"

She put out her hand to me, as if groping, her face still hidden. I held the hot hand tightly while the sobs grew less, and she struggled to command herself.

"Glad!" she said presently. "Glad! When a burden of misery is suddenly lifted glad is such a poor little word! My dear—my dear—what am I to say to you?"

"Why, nothing at all," I said, greatly relieved. "It was the very easiest little job, thanks to Judy and Jack. I had scarcely to do anything: they ran the launch, and I was a mere passenger. They were hugely delighted at the adventure."

"But will they say nothing?"

"They will not say a word, even to you. I have told them it is not a matter to be discussed; that the man on the Island was a friend we were helping, and that he wanted to get to Southport last night. I can trust Judy and Jack— when they have given their word nothing on earth can shake it. They understood that the matter was confided to them on condition that they should keep silent and ask no questions, and they are very proud of being trusted."

She drew a long breath.

"Sit down, and tell me everything that happened," she begged. "Every little detail."

I did so, touching very lightly on the rough journey home—hoping that she would not ask me if her brother had sent her any message. Probably she knew that a gentleman of Ronald Hull's type would have no thought for anyone but his precious self, for I had no awkward questions to dodge.

"It was all so simple and straightforward that there really is very little to tell," I finished. "I asked Mr. Hull not to speak in the boat, so that there would be no risk of the children's recognizing his voice: and I was so anxious to get back in case you needed me, that we didn't lose a moment. It was just a pleasure-trip. You don't mind that I took the children? Indeed, I meant to ask you, but you had gone to sleep before I could do it."

"I don't mind anything," she said. "There is no room in my heart for anything but the utmost relief and gratitude; how could there be when my burden is rolled away?" And she clung to my hand, and said a great many things I couldn't write down in cold blood—it made me feel an utter fool to listen to them. I only know I was very thankful when she stopped.

"Now, you are to go back to bed at once," she said. "Do not worry about me any more: you shall see how quickly I can get better now." And indeed, she looked almost like a girl, her cheeks flushed, and a light of happiness in her eyes. "Julia can do anything for me—she is very kind. I should be really glad if you would spend all day in bed."

One does not do such things if one is a governess-head-companion with buffering thrown in as a side-line. But I did sleep like a log until the dressing-gong boomed, and Judy and Jack pounded on my door begging me to go down for a swim. It gave one a thrill to run across the paddock as we had run the night before: to see the launch rocking lazily by the pier. Bence was busy in her. Jack scampered over to speak to him, dived in from the pier-head, and swam round to meet us, with his face one broad grin of impish joy.

"Bence is as wild as a meat-axe!" he said cheerfully. "Says it's no good cleaning out the launch every day when people 'liberately pour water into her at night! She really is awfully messy: that last big sea we shipped put gallons and gallons of water into her."

"What did you say to him?"

"I said it was a jolly shame," Jack chuckled. " 'Tis, too—poor old Bencey! I say, Miss Earle, haven't you got anyone for us to go out and rescue to-night?" He turned head-over-heels in the water, dived underneath Judy, and pulled her under by the leg. I left them arguing the matter out below the surface.

There was no holding my Fellow-Members of the Band that day. Their night adventure had left them wild with excitement; they rioted like mad things until I decided that exercise was the only possible treatment, packed up a billy and sandwiches, and took them out for a long day in the bush, leaving Mrs. McNab to the care of Julia, who liked nothing better than to have some one ill enough to be fussed over. Miles from home we came upon Dr. Firth, walking slowly through the scrub with his big Airedale at his heels. He looked gloomy enough before he saw us, but his face lit up when Judy and Jack hailed him joyfully.

"I was just deciding that treasure-hunting was a poor sort of game," he said. "This is about the tenth attempt I've made at scientific detective-work: I try to put myself in the position of a burglar leaving my house with his loot, desirous of avoiding all roads and tracks, and of finding a safe hiding-place until excited policemen have calmed down sufficiently to make it safe for him to get away. With this profound idea in our minds Sandy and I strike out across country and look for tracks!"

"I say—that's a jolly game!" cried Judy.

"It is quite a jolly game," he agreed. "Sandy entirely approves of it. It has given us a great deal of fresh air and exercise, and our health has benefited enormously—you can see for yourself how well Sandy looks!" He pulled the Airedale's ears. "But so far as finding the jewels goes, it doesn't seem to lead anywhere. That doesn't trouble Sandy, but it is hurtful to my pride. It would give me unbounded pleasure to be able to flourish my property before those two superior detectives, remarking airily, 'I told you so!'"

"I think you need help," Judy told him kindly. "Say we go with you and lend a hand?"

"Say I go with you, and forget all about the wretched old jewels," he responded. "I think it would do me good to have the cheerful society of you three merry people for a day. I don't seem to have had a moment free from the worry of them for the last week. By the way, my detectives have a fresh thrill; they went out boating before breakfast, and landed on Shepherd's Island."

Jack jumped, and Judy favoured him with a threatening glare.

"What's up, Jack?" inquired Dr. Firth.

"Trod on a stick," mumbled Jack, his face the colour of a beetroot. I felt that mine resembled it, and could only hope that Dr. Firth would put it down to sunburn.

But Judy did not turn a hair.

"What did they land for?" she inquired politely. "A picnic?"

"I think life is all a picnic to those two plump and worthy men," Dr. Firth responded. "I suppose they landed as a measure of exploration. They came back in some excitement, though, to breakfast—nothing makes my two sleuth-hounds forget their meals. A man has been camping in the old hut, they say: they found blankets there. Indeed, for all they know, he is still on the Island."

"But I suppose anyone may camp there?" I asked. "It isn't private property."

"Of course—dozens of people may use it, for all I know. However, the detectives have made up their minds that he is their man, and off they went after breakfast, to explore it thoroughly. I only hope they won't arrest some perfectly innocent holiday-maker and bring me his scalp!"

I did not dare to look at the children. They fell behind, affecting to examine a plant, and I heard smothered shrieks of glee. For myself, I found it difficult to listen to what my companion was saying: my brain was all a-whirl. If we had not gone last night——! And then I fell to wondering if anything that might be found on Shepherd's Island would bear marks that would be incriminating. The blankets, I knew, were plain Army grey ones; the food-tins, even if discovered, were only such as might be bought at any good store, and I knew Mrs. McNab had always ordered them from Melbourne. Ronald Hull would have hidden them carelessly: there was no hope that they would not be found by the detectives. Well, I could only hope that Mrs. McNab's prudence had guarded against supplying evidence. She had had long enough to practise prudence, poor soul.

We camped beside a little creek, boiled the billy, and shared our lunch with Dr. Firth; fortunately, I had learned that it was wise to provide amply for Judy and Jack's appetites, and there were plenty of sandwiches. Then Sandy dashed into the bush, to appear presently in triumph with a rabbit, which he laid at his master's feet. The sight of the little, limp body filled Judy and Jack with ambition to fish for yabbies, and Dr. Firth skilfully dissected a leg for each, while they tied strings to tea-tree sticks. Then they sat, supremely happy, on the bank, dangling their grisly baits, and drew up numbers of the hideous little fresh-water crayfish, which they stowed in the billy, with a view to supper. I had uneasy visions of Mrs. Winter's probable comments on the addition to her larder.

Dr. Firth and I sat under a tree, listening to their ecstatic yells, and talked. It was always easy to talk to him: each time we met seemed to show me more clearly what a friend I had found. Always he wanted to hear more and more of Colin and Madge, and of our life since we had lost Father; he knew all about the little Prahran flat, about Madge's music and her examination successes, and about Colin's dearness to us both. We laughed over our amateur housekeeping and over Colin's droll stories of his office—Colin had always made a joke of it, though Madge and I knew well enough how sorely he hated it. And then the talk would swing back to Father, and he would tell me stories of the youth they had spent together, until I felt that I knew Father better than I had ever done before, and had even greater cause for pride than I had dreamed of. The future, that had been so drab to us, seemed quite different now. Hardship and work there must be, of course, but not the loneliness that had walled us round since Father had gone away.

We had been so deeply engrossed that we had not noticed that the children had tired of fishing and had disappeared, leaving their rods on the bank beside the billy that was half full of squirming captives. I looked at my watch when we discovered their absence, and came back with a start to the realization of my duties.

"We ought to be making a move homeward," I said. "I don't want Mrs. McNab to be worried about us."

"Oh, they won't be far off," Dr. Firth said.

He sent a long coo-ee ringing through the scrub. A faint answering sound came, and following it, we went along the creek bank, to be greeted presently by the spectacle of Judy and Jack perched in a tree that partly overhung the water. Jack was feeling his way along a dead bough towards a hole that might or might not contain a parrot's nest. I cried out in alarm at sight of him, for the branch was rickety, and the ground below did not invite a fall—it was strewn with loose rocks, some of which had tumbled bodily into the creek.

"Do be careful, Jack!" I called. "That branch isn't safe."

"P'f! It's as safe as houses!" said Jack airily. "Don't bother a chap, Miss Earle—women are always fussy. I only want to get to this good old nest, and then I'll——"

There was a splintering crack and the branch sagged down suddenly. Jack clung to it for a moment while I ran towards him wildly; then he fell, as I made an ineffectual attempt to catch him. It failed, but it broke his fall. We went down to the ground together. A loose rock on the edge gave under us, and we rolled down the bank amid a scatter of stones and loose earth, ending with our feet in the creek.

We were both up in a moment, laughing. Dr. Firth's alarmed face peered over the bracken-fringed bank above us.

"Anyone hurt?"

"Nothing but a few scratches," I answered. "But we seem to have brought down half the bank—it's a regular avalanche. I don't believe we can get up there, Jack."

"Oh, can't we!" Jack uttered. "Bet you I can. I'll go ahead, Miss Earle, 'n' then I can pull you up."

"You needn't trouble," I thanked him. "I prefer a place where it's a little cleaner. Not that that matters much, since we rolled down!" I looked ruefully at my earth-stained frock.

"Well, I'll show you!" said Jack sturdily.

He scrambled up, sending down showers of small stones and loose soil, while I watched him, half expecting him to come sliding back to my feet. Just as he neared the top, my eye caught sight of a tiny object half hidden in our miniature avalanche—something that shone faintly. I stooped forward and picked up a bright sixpence.

"Take care, Jack—you are dropping your money," I called.

"Me?" inquired Jack, from the top. "Not me—I never had any. What's the use of bringing money out in the bush? Did you find any?"

"I found sixpence," I answered. "That's good luck for me, at all events. I wonder how it came here."

"Might be more lying about," suggested Jack. "Have a look."

I glanced up at him, laughing.

"If I find a silver-mine, I'll buy you that yacht you were talking about. What did you say her tonnage——?"

Something made me break off suddenly. There was a little recess in the bank, just under his laughing face: a recess only revealed since we had sent the rock that guarded it crashing down the bank. Something glimmered in it faintly. I went up the broken bank even more quickly than Jack had done, while the others sent a fire of laughing questions at me. Putting my hand into the recess I drew out—an old tobacco-tin.

"Whatever have you got there, Doris?" Dr. Firth asked.

"Somebody's 'baccy," I answered, laughing, scrambling up over the edge. "I suppose some poor old swagman has made a *cache* here. I must put it back."

"You might look at it first," he said quietly. But there was something in his voice that made me glance at his face. I sat down on the ground and got the lid open.

There was not tobacco inside, but moss—old soft moss, tightly rammed down. It might well have contained a fisherman's worms, but at the moment I didn't think of that, or I might not have acted as I did. I shook it all out, with a jerk, into my lap. Dr. Firth caught his breath in a gasp and the children gave a shout.

There was more than moss. Hidden among it were things that glittered and sparkled in the sunlight—rough-cut rubies and emeralds and sapphires, and softly-gleaming turquoises that bore the scratches of the tool that had hewn them hurriedly from their setting. They twinkled at us, lying among the soft bronze-green of the moss: Dr. Firth's stolen jewels! I sat and stared at them stupidly.

"You said they were magic!" shrilled Judy delightedly. "Oh, well done you, Miss Earle!"

"There should be more," said Dr. Firth quietly. "Pack them up again, Doris, and let us see where you found them."

We went over the edge in a body. There were two other little tobacco-tins in my hole, packed in the same way, stowed well under a rock. Half of it had broken away, and even then, only the smallest corner of the first tin had been visible—but for the lucky avalanche that Jack and I had brought down no one would ever have found that hiding-place, even if it had been years before the thief came back to remove his booty.

"I wouldn't have seen it at all if he had left the paper wrapping on the tin," I said. "It was the little gleam of metal that caught my eye."

"That was a small detail of extra carefulness," Dr. Firth said. "People have been tracked down before now by leaving something of which the purchase could be traced. He was a careful burglar, bless him!"

"He wasn't so smart when he dropped his sixpence!" exulted Jack. "It was the sixpence that started you looking, Miss Earle."

"It was. I was just turning away to look for a better place to get up when I saw it half under a stone."

"You ought to keep that sixpence for luck," said Judy solemnly. "Oh, Dr. Firth, are you going back to wave the jewels at the detectives? Do let us come too! I'd love to see their faces!"

"I shan't be in too much of a hurry," he said, smiling. "It might be as well to see what their new clue amounts to. Possibly there is something suspicious about that Shepherd's Island camper, after all."

My heart gave a sudden sick leap. What if there were?—if it had indeed been Ronald Hull who had hidden the jewels under the bank, trusting to luck some day to come back and retrieve them! What if his willingness to go to Adelaide were only a blind?—if he meant not to leave Australia at all, but only to get out of immediate danger here? I thought of poor Mrs. McNab's face that morning, ten years younger in her utter relief and thankfulness, and I shivered to think that her misery might not be over yet.

"We'll keep the matter to ourselves for a day or two, at any rate," Dr. Firth was saying. "You won't say a word, children?"

"Cross-our-hearts!" said Judy and Jack in chorus.

"That's all right. I'll see what the detectives have to say; and meanwhile I'll put a man of my own to watch this place, in case the man who planted those jewels comes back. Keep out of this part of the bush, you two, until I see you again."

They promised, wide-eyed. Life was indeed full of glory this week for little Judy and Jack McNab.

"But you won't wave them at the detectives without us?"

"Cross-my-heart!" said he solemnly. "I'll bring you and Miss Earle over, and you shall do the waving yourself, and see the sleuth-hounds collapse before you! And now, if you are ready, I think we'd better get home. I shall feel easier in my mind when these three tobacco-tins are locked away in my safe."

CHAPTER XVII
I USE A POKER

TO anyone who watched unseen, our progress homeward would undoubtedly have presented itself as peculiar. Dr. Firth's suggestion that the jewels would be more secure in his safe filled Judy and Jack with a vision of the thief coming to find his hidden booty. They scented danger in every clump of scrub, and earnestly demanded of Dr. Firth whether he had a revolver.

"Certainly I have—an excellent one," he answered. "It's in its case at home."

"Fancy you coming out to look for the jewels without it!" rebuked Judy. "I never heard of anything so careless. And if you meet the thief he's simply certain to be armed to the teeth!"

"I shall defy him to his teeth—even if false!" said the Doctor stoutly.

"Precious lot of good defying would be if he had a six-shooter!" growled Jack, who looked with a lofty scorn upon all literature that did not deal with the Far West. "Why, you're as good as a dead man if he gets the drop on you! I think each of us three ought to take a tobacco-tin and scoot—he'd never suspect any of us."

"It's a noble idea, but I like the feel of them in my pockets," responded the Doctor cheerfully. "I must e'en take my chance. Do you really think any modest burglar is going to be foolhardy enough to attack four desperadoes like ourselves—to say nothing of Sandy?"

"He'd pot you from behind a tree as soon as look at you," said Judy, with gloom. "Anyhow, Jack, you and me'll go ahead and scout. And you bring up the rear, Miss Earle—you might walk backwards as much as you can, in case he tries to stalk us from behind!"

We obeyed. Thus might have been seen two small forms flitting through the trees, peering in every direction: halting now and then, with lifted hand, to scan a possible danger-point: then, reassured, darting off to right or left, to reappear presently, perhaps examining a hollow stump, perhaps up a tree to obtain a wider view. In the rear, I endeavoured to be as sleuth-like as possible—dutifully walking backwards whenever I fancied they glanced in my direction, wherefore I twice sat down heavily on a tussock. In my next expedition of the kind the rear will be a position I shall carefully shun. Between our two forces, Dr. Firth stalked majestically, his chest thrown out, his hands clenched over his pockets—looking rather like Papa in *The Swiss Family Robinson*. Sandy was the only one of the party on whom life sat lightly. He hunted rabbits with a joyous freedom that I envied greatly.

We parted where the track branched off towards The Towers. Judy and Jack were profoundly uneasy at letting Dr. Firth continue his journey alone, preferring to risk the loss of their dinner rather than let him go home unguarded. It took all our persuasion, coupled with the reminder that their mother would certainly be worried about them, to induce them to say good-bye. They beguiled the way back to The Towers with the dreariest predictions of what might be expected to happen to him and the jewels deprived of their vigilance and mine.

We were very late for dinner, but Mrs. McNab had not worried. I do not think, that day, that she was capable of worrying. She was a different woman: there was a new light in her eyes, a little colour in her cheeks; her voice had lost the hard ring that had made it so repellent. Julia reported that she had taken her food like a Christian, and that you'd hardly know her, for the spirit she had on her. " 'Tis bein' forced away from the owld writin'," said Julia. "If I'd me way the divil a pen she'd see between now an' Patrick's Day!"

She made us sit in her room after dinner while the children told her about their day. It was nervous work, for the discovery of the jewels was naturally uppermost in their minds, and just as "all roads lead to Rome," so every topic we chose seemed only to merge into that crowning achievement of the day. Luckily, their mother was too blissfully content to notice occasional stumbling and hesitation. She gave them ready sympathy and outward attention, but I knew that half her mind was so busy rejoicing that she did not hear half they said.

As for Judy and Jack, they noticed nothing of her abstraction. They were only amazed at the change in her. I found them discussing it in bed when I went out on the balcony to tuck them in.

"Never knew Mother so jolly," said Jack. "Did you, Miss Earle? She was all smiling and int'rested—and generally about three minutes of us is all she can stick!"

"She looked so pretty, too," Judy added. "Her eyes were all big and soft. Miss Earle, you do really think she's better, don't you?" The child put her hand out and drew me down beside her. "She—she made me frightened," she said, with a catch in her voice. "You don't think she's going to be very ill, do you?"

"No, she isn't," I answered quickly—not sure of my own voice. "She's really ever so much better: in a few days she will be up. Mother has had a great deal of worry for a long time, old Fellow-Members, and now I hope that worry has gone."

Jack made a spring across from his bed and snuggled down beside Judy and me.

"Miss Earle—was the worry something to do with—with the job we helped you with last night?"

"Yes, it was. But you aren't going to ask questions."

"No, of course not. But I just wanted to know that much. It wasn't any harm just to ask that, was it?"

"No, indeed it wasn't, old man. You earned that, you and Judy."

"I'm glad I know," Judy said. "Will the worry ever come back! I do hope it won't, 'cause I'd love Mother to stay like she is now."

"I don't think it will," I said: I spoke stoutly, but again there was that sick fear at my heart. "It has been terribly hard for Mother to carry on, because she couldn't bear anyone but herself to have the worry."

"And things you keep to yourself are ever so much beastlier," observed Judy. "Do ask Mother to tell us, after you've gone, if it comes back, Miss Earle. We might be able to help."

"And anyhow, we'd take care of her," said Jack. "We'd make her a Member of the Band, if she'd like—only somehow, she's never seemed exactly Band-y before. She'd be a simply ripping Member if she stays like she is to-night!"

He gave a great yawn, stood up, and dived back to his own bed.

"I'm awful sleepy," he said. "But we've had two wonderful adventures, haven't we, Ju? These have been the best two days of my whole life!"

"Me, too," said Judy.

Would the worry ever come back! The fear was strong on me as I sat by my window before going to bed. Do as I might I could not shake off the feeling that Ronald Hull had not done with us yet. Why, I asked myself, should he go to America, when in Australia he had a sister ready to beggar herself and risk disgrace to protect him? And if this last dread were true—if it were he who had hidden the jewels in the hole under the bank of the creek—was it to be expected that he would leave the country without them? The evil face, with its cold eyes, seemed to hover before me in answer. Whatever happened, Ronald Hull would consider nobody in the world but himself.

I was very tired, and when I went to bed sleep came to me almost at once, and I dreamed a cheerful dream that Colin and I were chasing Mr. Hull across a paddock that ended in a precipice. We knew it was there, and so did he, and he tried to break back and escape; but Colin had not been a footballer for nothing, and he headed off every rush, countered every dodge, edging him on all the time: until at last Mr. Hull gave it up, and, running wildly and calling out unpleasant things, reached the edge of the cliff and sprang out in mid-air, twisting and turning as he fell, but never dropping his cigarette from his lips. He disappeared far below, and I woke up. I do not think it was a lady-like dream, but I felt astonishingly light-hearted. I knew how Sandy felt when he caught his rabbit.

I was just dropping off to sleep again when a sound fell upon my ears. It was so faint that at first I thought I was mistaken; then it came again, more distinctly, and I sat up, very wide-awake. Surely, some one was calling for help—a child's voice.

I sprang out of bed, flung on my dressing-gown and slippers, and ran out into the corridor. Something was happening downstairs: there was no light save that of the moon, but I heard a scuffle, and a man's voice, low and furious. And then another, and it was Jack's, crying, "Let go, you brute!" At that I lost my head altogether. Any sensible person would have summoned Harry McNab and his friends. But I fled downstairs without stopping to think, and, following the sounds, dashed into the library.

There were two figures there in the moonlight: Jack, in his pyjamas, a slight thing in the grip of a tall man who was trying to silence him. I heard an oath and a low-voiced threat, as I picked up the poker and struck at him. He let Jack go, turning on me savagely. I dodged his blow, struck again, and felt the blow go home: heard Jack crying out, "Look out, Miss Earle—he'll kill you!" It seemed very likely, as he rushed at me; but that was no reason for letting him kill Jack.

We circled round each other warily for a moment. Then he made another rush, and Jack sprang in between us and gripped him by the legs. He fell heavily over the boy: I sprang again, and hit wildly, caring not where I hit, and only wishing there were more strength in the blows. And then came another little figure—Judy, who flung herself across the struggling man, pounding wildly with her fists. I saw her thrown aside, and she did not move. Came racing feet, and the voice of Julia—"Let me at him, the murdherin' vilyun!" as I hit with my last ounce of strength, and staggered back.

"Sit on his head, Julia!" shrilled Jack.

"I will so," said Julia: and did.

I saw Jack crawling away, and flung myself across the struggling legs. We thrashed backwards and forwards on the floor, Julia keeping up a steady flow of threats, mingled with remarks addressed to the saints. And then the light was switched on, and the room was full of voices—men's voices, tense and angry. I could not see any of them: I was trying feebly to keep my hold, knowing I was done. Something like a thunderbolt caught the side of my head. Then came blackness and silence.

CHAPTER XVIII
I LOSE MY SITUATION

I REMEMBER a dream of pain that seemed to last for years: a dream in which lights flashed back and forth perpetually behind my eyes, and all the time there was a buzz of low voices; it troubled me greatly that I could never hear what they said. Then the dream faded, and there was something cool and wet on my forehead: I tried to tell them how good it was, but I seemed to have no tongue, so I gave up the attempt and went to sleep instead. And after years more of sleep I woke up in a room of dim twilight: and it was the most natural thing in the world to see Colin sitting beside my bed.

He saw my eyes open, and gave me his own old smile.

"Better, old girl?" He held something to my lips, and I drank thirstily.

"Is it time to start for school?" I whispered.

"Not nearly," he said. It was an immensely comforting statement to me. "Go to sleep again, kiddie." And I went obediently.

He was there the next time I awoke, but it was morning this time. They told me afterwards that for three days and nights he scarcely ever left my side, sitting just where I could see him if my eyes opened. No one could ever guess how beautiful it was to see him there. I grew to wondering would he still be there, before my heavy lids lifted: to be almost afraid to lift them, in case he should have gone away. But always his smile was ready for me, and I would drift away to sleep again, trying to smile back.

Then one day I woke up with my brain quite clear, and the desire for sleep all gone. Colin put his fingers on my wrist, and I lay watching a little ray of sunlight that crept in by the blind and fell across his crisp hair. He did not take his eyes from me, but spoke to some one I could not see.

"All right," he said quietly. "Come along and say good morning to her, Madge."

Madge came—which also seemed a most natural thing. She kissed me very gently and stood back with her hand on Colin's shoulder, and I grinned foolishly at them both.

"I've had a tremendous sleep," I said, "and all sorts of queer dreams. And I'm ever so hungry!"

"That's much better to think about than the dreams," said Colin. He put out a long arm and mysteriously produced some jelly, with which he fed me like a baby. It was wonderfully good, and I ate six spoonfuls, and then discovered that I wasn't as hungry as I had thought. So I went to sleep again, holding a hand of each.

It was quite a long while before they would let me talk about what had happened in the library. They thought I did not remember much about it at first, which was quite wrong: I remembered everything until the stunning blow that put me out of action. But I did not know what I dared ask. You see, I had never seen the thief's face clearly, but his height and build were the same as Ronald Hull's. In my mind, as I lay finding my strength again, I was quite sure that that estimable gentleman had returned to pick up a little more loot.

Judy and Jack were safe—I knew that, because they came and peeped at me every day and brought me flowers. And Julia also: she swept and polished my room, and showed much hatred and jealousy of the stern little trained nurse who wouldn't let her do the dusting. But when I asked feebly for Mrs. McNab they told me she was still too ill to get up; the shock of the attempted robbery at The Towers had evidently made her worse. So I held my peace as best I could, outwardly, though in my mind I ached to know if Ronald Hull were the individual I had so heartily battered with the poker. If so—well, I trembled for Mrs. McNab, but I was glad I had done the battering.

Then, one day, Mrs. McNab came in, in her dressing-gown, looking like a tall ghost: and Colin slipped out and left us alone. She kissed me and sat down by my bed.

"Tell me——" I whispered.

"Tell you what, my dear?" She bent towards me.

"Did they get him?"

"Whom do you mean, Doris dear?" She looked puzzled.

"Your brother. Did the police get him?"

A great relief flashed into her face.

"Ronald! Oh no. He got quite safely away from Adelaide. His friend wrote to me after the ship had sailed: there had been no difficulty at all. That worry is ended, thank God!"

"Oh!" I said weakly. "Then it wasn't he—in the library? I thought it was."

"In the library? You—you don't mean the burglar? Why, my dear child, that was Bence!"

"Bence! Not the chauffeur?" Bence had always been especially civil to me. I felt a guilty pang, remembering how hard I had tried to hit him with the poker.

"Yes, it was Bence. He turned out to be a very well-known criminal—the police had been looking for him for some time. He was responsible for all the robberies; some of Dr. Firth's property was found in his room, in addition to the jewels you children discovered in the bush. He has made a full confession." She looked at me doubtfully. "Will it excite you to hear about it?"

"It will excite me far more *not* to hear," I said truthfully. "I've been lying here for days, aching to see you: there was no one else I dared to ask. Do tell me. Did I hit him very hard?"

"You got in one lucky blow that dazed him, and a good many that hurt him a good deal. But for that I do not know what would have happened to you and the children. As it was, Julia seems to have arrived just in time, for he was getting his wits back. I don't know that anyone is certain of what actually happened—you were all struggling in the darkness, and Judy was stunned. But just as Harry and Dicky arrived and turned on the lights he kicked you with tremendous force on the head: I don't know whether he meant it, or if it were done blindly in his struggles."

"I think it must have been that," I said. "Bence was always very courteous!"

Mrs. McNab gave a short laugh.

"He was past being courteous just then. The blow sent you flying, and the other side of your head crashed into the carved leg of a table. Then, of course, the boys mastered him easily enough, aided by Julia, who fought with great fury. He was rather badly knocked about—they were all beside themselves, seeing you and Judy unconscious. Judy was quite well in half an hour. But you have been a more serious matter—though we shall soon have you as strong as ever." And then she put her grey head down on my hand, and I felt it wet with her tears.

"And you got Colin and Madge for me! That was ever so dear of you."

"That was the least we could do. Dr. Firth managed it for us: they were here next day. I think they rather wanted to kill us all at first, but they have forgiven us now. I have told Colin everything, Doris—about my brother and Shepherd's Island. It was right that he should know. And though he was naturally distressed at all that you have undergone, I do not think he blames me—perhaps not as much as I blame myself. 'I don't see what else you could have done,' he said. He has been wonderfully kind to me. It is easy to see why you are so proud of him."

"Well—yes," I said. "There never was anyone like Colin."

She smiled at me.

"Colin seems to have the same conviction about you," she said. "Here he comes: I am told he is terribly stern if your visitors stay too long. Julia says he is the one person of whom the nurse is afraid!"

Colin came in and stood at the foot of the bed, very tall and good to look at. We laughed at each other.

"I thought my patient might be tired," he said. "But you are doing her good, Mrs. McNab."

"I was worrying over something that Mrs. McNab has explained to me," I said. "Now I shan't worry any more. Colin, isn't it a good thing you made me practise boxing with you? I should never have landed my best efforts on Bence if it hadn't been for that!"

He stared at me.

"Why, I thought you had forgotten all about it," he said. "Have you been lying there gloating in secret over your savagery?"

"Something like that," I laughed. "I feel I ought to have done better—but a dressing-gown does cramp one's style with a poker!"

He laughed too, but there was something in his eyes that brought a lump into my throat.

"You blessed old kid!" he said softly. That was a good deal for Colin to say, and it told me more than if anyone else had talked for a week.

They brought me downstairs a few days later, looking very interesting in a wonderful blue teagown that Mrs. McNab had ordered for me from Melbourne. Colin carried me, for my knees still bent under me in the most disconcerting fashion when I tried to walk, and put me on a lounge in the garden, with a rug over my feet. Most of the house-party had gone away, but there were enough left to make quite a crowd, after my quiet time in my room, and they all made a ridiculous fuss over me. Dicky Atherton and Harry McNab plied me with unlimited offers of food. Even Beryl was quite human; she brought me my tea herself, and actually ran for an extra cushion. It was all very disconcerting, but when I got used to it, it was lovely to be outside again. Judy and Jack had planted a huge Union Jack at the head of my couch. They sat down, one on either side of me, and declined to yield their positions to anyone. "You may think you own her," Judy said to Colin, her nose in the air. "But we're the Band!"

It was some days after when they took me out for my first drive. I could walk now, and I was dressed, even though Madge did say my clothes looked as if they were draped on a bean-pole: but they still took great care of me, and anyone would have thought I was really important, to see how Julia tucked the rug round me and slipped a little soft pillow behind my back. " 'Tis lookin' well ye are, thank God!" she said, regarding the effect judicially. "Let ye go aisy, now, over the bumps, sir. There's a pot-hole in the road beyant, that Bence druv me into wan time; an' 'twas a mercy the lid was on the car, or it's out I'd have been. I have the bump on me head yet!"

"I will, Julia," said Colin, at the wheel. "Quite ready, Mrs. McNab?" as she took her place beside me. "Hop in, Madge." We slid off gently, leaving Julia waving from the steps.

I don't think I'll ever forget that first drive. The country was all dried-up, for no rain had fallen for weeks: but even the yellow paddocks were beautiful to me, and every big red-gum tree seemed to welcome me back. As we mounted the headland above Porpoise Bay the sea came in sight, blue and peaceful, with little flecks of white foam far out, and here and there the brown sails of a fishing-boat. The islands were like jewels on its bosom. I looked at the green hills of Shepherd's Island, and thought of the night—how long ago it seemed!—when the children and I had taken off our silent passenger, and of how narrowly we had escaped running upon its rocks as we raced home before the driving storm. It had been a wild enough venture, but it had succeeded; and it had given me the two best little comrades anyone need want. Never were allies stauncher than my Fellow-Members of the Band.

The drive was only a short one: Dr. Firth had asked us to afternoon tea, saying that the distance was quite long enough for my first outing. He seemed curiously young and happy as he ran down the steps to meet us. Already he and Colin and Madge were firm friends. I liked to watch him whenever his eyes rested on Colin. They made me think of Father's eyes, full of pride in a son.

The housekeeper came out to welcome me, and we had tea in the verandah, among the ferns and palms. After we had finished, Mrs. McNab took out her knitting and settled herself comfortably in a lounge-chair.

"I know you want to show these children the house," she said. "I will sit here, if you don't mind, Dr. Firth. Be sure you do not let Doris become tired. I heard her tell Colin this morning that her knees were still 'groggy.' Of course, I can only guess at the meaning of that expression—still——!" She laughed at me as I pulled down the corners of my mouth.

"I'm afraid I'm pretty hopeless as a governess," I said contritely.

"So hopeless that I fear we'll have to find you other occupation," said the Doctor, laughing. He patted my shoulder. "Come and give me your opinion of my spring-cleaning."

The big house was very different now. The rooms that had been full of cabinets and showcases were re-furnished: one a billiard-room, with a splendid new table, the other a very charming sitting-room, dainty, yet homelike, with comfortable chairs and couches, a piano, a writing-table, and low book-cases full of enticing-looking books. I exclaimed at it.

"What a jolly room!"

"This is a home-y room, I think," the Doctor said, looking round it with satisfaction. "The drawing-room is too big and gorgeous for ordinary use: I'm afraid of it. Later on I may become brave enough to go into it, but it needs to be furnished with dozens of people. Oh, well, perhaps that can be arranged in time. Now come and see where the wild beasts lived."

There were no grim beasts and reptiles now. Instead, the room was bare, with a shining new floor—a floor that instinctively made one's feet long to dance. There was a little stage at one end for musicians: big couches near the walls, where hung some fine old paintings. A double door opened into a long conservatory. And that was all.

"Oh, what a ballroom!" Madge cried.

"Will it do?" he said.

"I should think it will! Isn't it just perfect, Doris?"

"It is, indeed," I said. "Do ask us to come when you give a ball, Dr. Firth."

"I will—if you will promise to give me the first dance. After that I'll let the youngsters have a chance, and take my place meekly with the aged; but the first dance is my perquisite. Now I want to show you some other rooms. Is she strong enough for the stairs, do you think, Colin?"

"Not to be thought of, with groggy knees!" said my brother. He picked me up as if I were a baby and strode upstairs with me, disregarding my protests.

"Yes, you're putting on a little weight," he said, setting me gently on the landing. "Nothing to speak of, of course, but you're rather more noticeable to carry than you were a week ago—upstairs, at any rate. Where next, sir?"

"Here," said the Doctor.

He led us into one bedroom after another. A man's room first, with a little iron bedstead, big chairs, a heavy writing-table and book-cases, and plenty of space. Next, a dainty room, all furnished in pink, where roses sprawled in clusters on the deep cream ground of an exquisite French wall-paper. From it opened a bare, panelled room, the sole furniture of which was a grand piano and three chairs.

"Why, that's the twin to your Bechstein, Madge!" I said.

Madge astonished me by suddenly turning scarlet.

"Is it?" she said awkwardly.

"Don't stay to argue over pianos," Dr. Firth said. "There's another room to see."

It was a very lovely room. A little carved bed stood in an alcove under a broad casement-window; all the colouring was delicate blue and grey, and it was full of air and sunlight. The furniture was of beautiful grey silky-oak: the chintzes were faintly splashed with pink here and there, and there was pink in the cushions on the great Chesterfield couch. Never, I think, was there so dainty a room.

"One has to ask a lady's permission before one sits down in her room," said Dr. Firth, with a twinkle. "May we sit down in your apartment, Doris?"

"Mine?" I stammered. And then I saw Colin's face, and I knew there was something I had not been told.

Colin came with one stride, and put me on the big couch.

"Listen, Dor, old girl," he said. "Dr. Firth has been making great plans: he's such a strenuous planner that it isn't the least bit of use to argue with him, I find. They are very wonderful plans for us." And then the big fellow fairly choked. "I think you'd better go on, sir," he managed to say.

"I'm a very lonely man, Doris," the Doctor said. "I've no one belonging to me in the world, and far too much money for one man to use. And you three are the children of the best friend I ever had, to whom, at one time, I owed everything. Wherefore, I am about to adopt you. I may say, I have already adopted you. I don't know how one does it legally, but I'm very sure no one is going to get you away from me."

I could only look from him to Colin: and Colin's face was very grave and very happy. So I knew it was all right.

"Colin is a stiff-necked person," the Doctor went on. "I have had most tiring arguments with him, thanks to his abominable pride. Thank goodness, I think I have succeeded in making him see that Denis Earle's son, cut out for a doctor if ever a fellow was, is thrown away in an insurance office. As a matter of principle, it is all wrong. So Colin is going back to the University to take his degree——"

"Oh!" I cried. "Colin—Colin!" I put my head against his coat and simply howled. He held me very tightly. I believe he wasn't much better himself, big as he is.

"Madge is going to be a boarder for a couple of years. Personally, I don't want her to be a very learned lady and fag herself to a shadow with innumerable examinations; but as to that, you three must settle the matter and do as you think best. But she can go as far as she likes with her music, with my full approval, if only she'll come home here and play to me on her Bechstein whenever she gets a chance."

Madge was perched on the arm of his chair. She leaned across and kissed the top of his head airily.

"Thank you," said the Doctor. "I believe we can consider that signed and sealed. As for you, we have told Madame Carr that she can find some one else for her twelve-year-olds. I want some one to look after me and make this place the sort of home we want it to be whenever Colin and Madge can come back to us. It's only a house at present, but I rather think it will be a home when you are here."

"And you can't argue, Dor," Madge said wildly. " 'Cause we've sub-let the flat in Prahran!" She hurled herself on me. "Say you'll agree, Dor. It's going to be just perfect!"

I looked at Colin.

"It's for you to say," he said. "I'll do whatever you like, old Dor. I wasn't tired of your housekeeping, you know—only of seeing you at it." He gave a big sigh. "To think of you in a place like this—not tired and worried any more!"

"To think of you," I said—"with your degree. Not washing saucepans?"

"Then may we call it a bargain?" the Doctor said.

I went over to him and kissed him just where Madge had kissed him.

"Signed and sealed," he said contentedly.

Milton Keynes UK
Ingram Content Group UK Ltd.
UKHW010802110624
444053UK00004B/413